# ON THE EDGE

". . . absolutely certain about this, Mr. Higgins?"

"There's no question, Mr. President. I just spoke with General Cord. We served in SOG together and there was a time when Zach and I were very close. And for the sake of that old friendship, he just warned me to pack my bags and get out of town."

"He actually said that?"

"Word for word. Sir, he's apparently gone far enough that he's got nothing to hide anymore. If the government won't accede to his demands, he can launch missiles from Warren Air Force Base and target New York, or Boston, or Chicago, or any other city that he chooses to make an example of. And he knows there's practically nothing we can do to stop him."

*Books by J. D. Masters*

**STEELE
COLD STEELE
KILLER STEELE
JAGGED STEELE**

**RENEGADE STEELE**
*(coming in September)*

# JAGGED STEELE

## J. D. MASTERS

CHARTER BOOKS, NEW YORK

JAGGED STEELE

A Charter Book/published by arrangement with
the author

PRINTING HISTORY
Charter edition/June 1990

All rights reserved.
Copyright © 1990 by Charter Communications, Inc.
This book may not be reproduced in whole
or in part, by mimeograph or any other means,
without permission. For information address: The Berkley
Publishing Group, 200 Madison Avenue, New York, New York 10016.

ISBN: 1-55773-346-5

Charter Books are published by The Berkley Publishing Group,
200 Madison Avenue, New York, New York 10016.
The name "CHARTER" and the "C" logo
are trademarks belonging to Charter Communications, Inc.

PRINTED IN THE UNITED STATES OF AMERICA

10  9  8  7  6  5  4  3  2  1

For Ed Bryant,
with friendship and affection

# 1

Oliver Higgins, his elegantly tailored suit freshly pressed and his graying hair carefully combed, took his seat behind the table and pulled the mike over in front of him. He straightened his silk foulard tie, glanced up nervously at the members of the subcommittee and moistened his lips. He poured himself a glass of water from the carafe on the table, took a sip and waited for the hammer to fall.

"Thank you for coming, Mr. Higgins." Senator Carman, the chairman, sat in the center of the raised dais flanked by the other members of the subcommittee. Having greeted him, he then looked down and started leafing through the report before him, ignoring him completely.

He was in his early sixties, heavyset, with a thick shock of snow white hair and bright blue eyes. He looked like an amiable Irish uncle and he spoke softly, with a touch of gravel in his voice, but Higgins knew that his polite and charming manner was deceiving. Carman could make or break him. The senator from Massachusetts was one of the most influential legislators in Congress, chairman of both the Armed Services and the

Ways and Means Committees. He was one of the people who controlled the pursestrings, and he made no secret of his dislike for the CIA.

Carman felt that the agency had outlived its usefulness. In the days before the Bio War, there had been a pressing need for gathering intelligence concerning the operations of foreign governments, but now most of those governments had either collapsed or were hanging by a thread, including the crippled government of what was left of the United States.

The genetically engineered plague that had been released upon the world by Islamic terrorists and the brief, aborted nuclear exchange that followed it had wiped out almost three-quarters of the world's population. Most surviving governments were too busy trying to control the anarchy within their own borders to concern themselves with what was happening in other countries. It would be a long time before any government grew strong enough to pose a threat to other nations. There was a limited amount of contact, a foreign policy predicated on mutual survival and reorganization, but by and large, isolationism was the order of the day.

With Washington, D.C., reduced to a huge puddle of radioactive glass, the federal government had moved to New York City. What had once been the UN Secretariat Building, the tall glass slab that rose up over the East River, now housed the administrative offices of Congress and various federal agencies, the CIA among them. The President resided on the thirty-seventh floor. The General Assembly Building, the smaller, saddle-shaped structure adjoining the Secretariat, now housed the Congress of the United States, and Higgins sat in one of its quiet, plenary meeting rooms.

Not all fifty states were represented in Congress. There were no representatives from Alaska, Hawaii, Texas or Nevada. Perhaps survivors still existed in Alaska and Hawaii, but there was no functioning authority in either state. As for Nevada, most of it was still too hot for anyone to enter safely, and following the war, Texas had seceded from the union to form its own republic. All efforts to bring it back into the fold had thus far met with failure.

After the plague had been released, the superpowers had ordered retaliatory strikes, each thinking that the other was responsible. However, only a small portion of the world's nuclear arsenal was actually launched. Missile control personnel had keeled over at their consoles and died with their fingers poised over the buttons, leaving the missiles still standing in launch mode in their silos. Strikes had occurred, but not all designated targets had been hit. Moscow and London were both gone. Paris had been partially reduced to rubble. Peking was nuked into oblivion.

Isolated strikes had occurred throughout Europe, Asia and the United States. South America, the African continent, Australia, Greenland, Canada and Mexico, most of Southeast Asia, the Scandinavian countries and Japan had escaped the fire, but they had not escaped unscathed. The rapidly spreading airborne plague had done its work, decimating the defenseless populations as the virus went through its series of mutations before it finally reached the end of its cycle.

The government of the United States, what remained of it, was headquartered in New York, with branches in Boston, Philadelphia, Detroit, and other cities. The Supreme Court sat in Chicago. The Joint Chiefs of Staff were based in Atlanta, and other government departments were spread throughout the Midwest and along the Eastern Seaboard in various urban centers. This strange decentralization was partly a function of postwar paranoia and partly an effort to maintain control in civilized areas.

Florida had become a modern-day version of the Dry Tortugas, a semi-independent state with its corrupt capitol in Miami, a haven for pirates from the Gulf and the Caribbean, as well as every other criminal, hustler and freebooter from Savannah to the Florida Keys. Most of the Southwest, with the exception of cities such as Phoenix, Santa Fe and Albuquerque, had regressed to the frontier lifestyle of the 1800's. The northwest and the mountain states had been the hardest hit. There were still hot spots in Idaho, Montana, Utah, Colorado and Wyoming, as well as the Dakotas. Isolated pockets of civilization existed in Washington State and Oregon, but California had been devastated. The strikes out there had triggered off the Big One and the Golden State now had a radically different coastline.

New York City had collapsed into itself like a dying star.

Midtown Manhattan had escaped destruction, but the southernmost tip of Manhattan, once the home of the financial district, was now a rubble of twisted steel, shattered glass and crumbled concrete. Out in New York Harbor, the Statue of Liberty had been reduced to molten slag and hardly anything remained of Staten Island. The Bronx was like a DMZ, largely deserted, and much of Long Island was a ghost town, with the surviving settlements under the control of several large, heavily fortified and well-organized criminal enclaves. Miniature mob kingdoms ruled Queens, Brooklyn and Long Beach. The government had managed to topple one of them, the powerful Borodini Enclave on the north shore in Cold Spring Harbor, but the others still operated like independent city-states, drawing on the freebooters plying the Atlantic Coast for their supplies, as well as the agro-communes and the fishing fleets operated by The Brood, a large gang of outlaw bikers who had seized control of the far eastern end of the island.

On Manhattan Island, everything south of Houston Street and east of Second Avenue up to 34th Street, as well as the entire strip along the Hudson River from Battery Park to the collapsed Lincoln Tunnel, was a lawless no-man's-land populated by derelicts, outlaws and para-military street gangs that controlled the shaky economy of the slums and ruled its poverty-stricken residents. Everything north of 110th Street was a decimated ghetto, primarily under the control of a powerful black street gang called the Skulls. What had once been the greatest city in the world now had its mass densely clustered at the center, a core city surrounded by a twilight zone of urban jungle.

It was the same throughout much of the country. Initially the survivors had fled the cities in droves, but they had found the rural areas well defended by farmers, ranchers and small town citizens for whom guns and hunting had been a way of life. Many of them were outdoorsmen and gun collectors, others were survivalists whose worst nightmares had come true. They were well prepared to defend their homes from the hordes of hungry, frightened, desperate people who had fled the cities. And those who had spent their lives in pampered urban comfort soon discovered that they were very ill equipped to survive outside the environs of the cities. Before long, the survivors started drifting back, to once more make their homes in cities that suddenly had no shortage of accommodations, where they could depend at least to some degree upon the overworked authorities who struggled to restore some semblance of law and order as they tried to revitalize a crippled economy and feed their starving citizens.

Slowly, society stumbled back to its feet, but it was still staggering and weaving like a battered prizefighter in the final round. The police forces patrolled the crime-ridden streets like British commandos had once patrolled the streets of Ulster, dressed for combat and armed with automatic weapons. The military had their hands full trying to restore order to the outlying areas and protecting the farm settlements that had been reorganized as agro-communes, supplying the hungry cities by means of well-armed military convoys.

The social order had become surreal. In the core cities, people lived and worked and voted and paid taxes, but there were few who didn't own and carry guns. And despite the stressful temper of the times, there were nowhere near as many shootings as might have been expected. An armed society was a *polite* society and that politeness was enforced not only by police, but also by a growth industry in personal security. Numerous private concerns, regulated by the police, contracted with building and block associations, as well as businesses, to provide armed guards for the protection of the premises.

Yet on the fringes of the cities, in the slums and what were once the wealthy suburbs, what little order and economy existed was administered by outlaw gangs that often competed with each other for control. The police patrolled the borders of the cities and sought to gradually extend them, block by block and street by street. But all too often, they would bring one small piece of no-man's-land under their control only to have another area ignite. And once they'd dealt with that, they found the gangs back in control of the area that they had just subdued.

As for the remainder of the country, the rural areas, the small towns and the villages were largely on their own. Here and there, in the more populated regions, National Guard units, augmented by local police and citizenry, protected the towns from bands of savage raiders that roamed the devastated countryside. Elsewhere, vigilante justice was the law. Some local governments, such as they were, maintained contact with federal authorities, others pointedly avoided it, distrusting the government that they blamed for bringing them to such a state.

Texas was the prime example. They had been spared the missile strikes, but not the ravages of the plague, and with only the shallow Rio Grande separating them from Mexico, they felt they had enough problems of their own without having to concern themselves with those of the rest of the country. Their solution had been elegantly simple. They formed their own republic, with a new capitol in Dallas, and they closed all their borders *except* the one on the Mexican side. As a result, they had a steady influx of cheap labor to help maintain their own economy and their influence extended well beyond the Rio Grande. They traded with the freebooters in the Gulf and eliminated problems with narcotics by legalizing drugs. They maintained diplomatic relations with the federal government, but they had no desire to subject themselves to its authority. They were doing better on their own. And legislators like Senator Bryce Carman were painfully aware that Texas stood as a dangerous example to the other states. The tax base, such as it was, was pathetically inadequate to the task of getting the country back on its feet once more. Military units often went for months without receiving any pay, and there were frequent problems with keeping the troops under control.

Carman and the other members of the subcommittee had become, out of necessity, legislative hatchet men. With a crippled government forced to operate on a shoestring budget, they had to cut wherever possible and Higgins knew that one of the areas Carman wanted to cut most was the already pared-down budget of the CIA.

The agency was, in Carman's view, a dinosaur that had outlived its time. Royce Harding, the agency director, had already seen the writing on the wall. He had submitted meekly to the knife each time he was brought before Carman's committee. He hadn't even bothered to insist upon attending when Higgins was summoned to appear before them. He was already thinking of the next post that Carman could help him to secure if he played ball. Higgins alone, as the director of the agency's Project Download and its subsidiary, Project Steele, was the sole remaining reason for a budgetary allocation. He had managed to keep it afloat only because the project had proved so successful.

They had demonstrated that it was possible for people to use biochips implanted in their brains to interface directly with computers. It allowed them to download vital knowledge and abilities that could then be programmed into others, thereby saving untold effort and expense in training important personnel. A direct outgrowth of that process had been Project Steele, a man with sophisticated nysteel alloy prosthetics incorporating weapons systems and a cybernetic brain programmed with human mental engrams. Lt. Donovan Steele was a cyborg, a prototype of the weapon of the future, capable of doing the work of over a dozen highly trained military or police personnel. Steele's performance had been so outstanding that even Carman was impressed and had voted to continue with the funding, enabling them to proceed with Project Stalker, a second generation cyborg. But now the project had been dealt a staggering setback. Perhaps even a mortal blow.

Stalker went insane as soon as he was brought on line. He had murdered his creators and gone on a killing spree throughout the city before Steele finally destroyed him. Now, as Higgins sat and waited while Carman and his fellow subcommittee members consulted the reports before them, he knew that in a matter of moments, he would be fighting for his life.

"I'm sure we don't need to tell you why you're here, Mr. Higgins," Carman began, still looking down and leafing through the report. "The last time you appeared before this subcommittee, you assured us that your project was an unqualified success and that you had ironed out any and all potential difficulties inherent in the process of producing cyborgs." He paused and fixed Higgins with an unwavering stare. "Isn't that correct?"

Higgins cleared his throat. "Yes, sir, I did say that. However—"

"However," Carman interrupted, "as it turns out, there were still some rather significant difficulties that had not been as you put it, 'ironed out.' Difficulties that were graphically demonstrated in Project Stalker, your second generation cyborg. And using the term 'difficulties' in this case is rather an understatement, wouldn't you agree?"

Higgins did not respond.

"Nothing to say, Mr. Higgins?" Carman said, raising his bushy white eyebrows.

"I'm sorry, sir, I had assumed it was a rhetorical question," Higgins said. "However, I would tend to agree that the word 'difficulties' might be an understatement, considering the way you put it."

"Oh? And how would *you* put it, Mr. Higgins?"

"I'd say it was largely a matter of perspective, sir."

"Perspective? Really? Would you care to explain that?"

"Yes, sir, I would. Looking at it from the standpoint of what resulted, which is to say, considering what happened from the perspective of purely subjective, human terms, I'd say that the word 'tragedy' would be much more appropriate. However, when you examine the situation from a strictly scientific perspective, the word 'difficulties' would not by any means be an understatement."

"Under the circumstances, Mr. Higgins," Carman said dryly, "I find your taking refuge in semantics in this manner in poor taste and wholly inappropriate."

"With all due respect, sir, it's not a matter of semantics. And I'd appreciate the opportunity to clarify that statement."

"By all means, please do," said Carman with a wry grimace. "This committee has already been misled enough. We would greatly appreciate clarification in this matter."

"Yes, sir. To begin, I'd like to state for the record that there was never any attempt on my part or on the part of any of the project staff to mislead this committee. My original report to this committee was and *is* correct. We *have* successfully eliminated all the technical problems inherent in the process of producing cyborgs. The process works. The prosthetics and the cybernetic systems involved, in both Project Steele and Project Stalker, functioned flawlessly throughout. In both cases, the process of downloading mental engrams from the human brain and the subsequent loading of those engrams into a cybernetic brain worked perfectly. Technically, there *were* no problems. However, we're not dealing with a strictly technical situation here. We're also dealing with the human factor.

"In both cases," Higgins continued, "the subjects had experienced brain damage prior to being cyborged. As a result, in each case, it was necessary to supplement the engram matrix with ancillary data obtained during prior downloading test runs with other subjects. The details are covered in the report. This supplementary data was incorporated into the engram matrix to make up for the damage resulting from the subjects' injuries. In the case of Project Steele, it did not in any way interfere with the subject's ability to function, as you have observed yourselves. In the case of Project Stalker, the brain damage was apparently much more severe. It's also possible that the subject had some prior existing psychological problems inherent in his personality."

"Just a moment, Mr. Higgins," said Roberta Dillingsworth, the senator from Pennsylvania. "Let me get this straight. Are you trying to claim that your second cyborg went out of control because he was insane to begin with?"

"No, ma'am, not exactly. That would be an oversimplification," Higgins replied.

"It sounds more like obfuscation to me," said Dillingsworth, with a frown. "We have complete files on both men, *including* their psychological profiles. And in neither case are any psychological problems indicated."

"Yes, ma'am, that's quite true," said Higgins. "However, both subjects were veteran NYPD Strike Force officers, and in that capacity, they were subject to regular and frequent psychiatric evaluations. As police psychiatrists will readily attest, officers tend to resent these periodic evaluations. They come to believe, not without some justification, that the department shrinks are looking for the least excuse to remove them from active Strike Force duty. They become cautious and defensive. The longer they remain on the force, the more adept they become at playing what they call 'the game,' concealing their true feelings and trying to outwit their examiners. An officer with emotional problems would never seek help from a police psychiatrist for fear of being removed from duty. There are, unfortunately, many documented cases where such problems were never revealed until they resulted in a tragic breakdown, a psychosis or a suicide. These men often build up walls and hide their innermost feelings, even from their wives. In other words, the fact that their psychological profiles don't indicate any problems doesn't necessarily mean that they weren't there.

The fact remains that we followed the same basic procedure with both cyborgs. The first one experienced no problems and remains perfectly functional in all respects. The second went insane and had to be destroyed. And that task was accomplished by Lt. Steele, which should clearly demonstrate his capabilities.

"My point," he concluded, "is that the fault does not lie with the process, which works and works extremely well. The only variable factor we're looking at here is that of human personality. To put it another way, if one soldier has a breakdown and becomes psychotic, you don't disband the entire army, do you?"

Dillingsworth pursed her lips thoughtfully and nodded. And looking at the other members of the committee, Higgins could see he'd made his point, even if he had stretched the truth a little. Carman frowned.

"I'd also like to reiterate," said Higgins quickly, striking while the iron was still hot, "that the production of cyborgs is only a byproduct of what Project Download is really all about. An important byproduct, but a byproduct nonetheless. We're suffering from a drastic shortage of trained personnel. Given enough funding, we'll be able to utilize the process to remedy that situation. And it isn't a question of *if* we can do it, it's a question of *when*. All of our preliminary experiments have resulted in dramatic successes. Right now, we can take a download from a highly trained soldier implanted with a biochip and create a program that will allow us to produce as many soldiers of equal capabilities as we can manufacture biochips for. And we can do it in a fraction of the time that it would take to train them normally. We could do the same thing with police officers, technicians, teachers, scientists, any needed occupation."

"Even politicians?" said Carman with a smile.

Higgins didn't fall into the trap. "Well, some abilities are more subtle and refined than others," he said offhandedly, so it wouldn't sound like he was stroking them. "Leadership, for example, is more a function of the personality than learned abilities. And the chief aim of the project is to enhance human learning ability by means of computer technology. Obviously, it would be much more difficult to pass on leadership potential than, say, combat skills or technical knowledge. Chances are it may not even be possible. However, that's not what we're concerned with. We can't alter human personality," he said, knowing full well that they could do precisely that, "but we *can* pass on human skills and knowledge. And that alone can revolutionize society and help us pull this country back together. I realize that you're under extremely tight budgetary constraints, but continued funding of the project will enable you to save a tremendous amount of money in the long run. Additionally, cyborgs can free up a lot of personnel for more necessary tasks. Our work is vital and imperative. Cutting our funding at this stage would be like killing off the goose that lays the golden eggs."

"I won't quibble with the fact that you lay eggs," said Carman dryly, "but I'm not convinced they're made of gold. In fact, some of them seem downright poisonous. Project Stalker was a particular case in point. A lot of lives were lost as a result. The people are holding us accountable. They want assurances that such a thing will not occur again and it's our responsibility to give them those assurances. Frankly, Mr. Higgins, you haven't said anything that leads me to believe that you can guarantee it won't happen again."

"Sir, I—"

"I haven't finished," Carman said, "I'm inclined to agree with you that Project Download is addressing a real and very present need. However, I don't believe that cyborgs are a part of it. Using computer technology to improve human learning ability is one thing. Using that same technology to create people that are part machine is something else entirely. It's extremely controversial, incredibly expensive, and, what's more, as we have already seen, it can be highly dangerous. And I think this world is already dangerous enough. We'll have to deliberate on this, but it's going to be my recommendation to this subcommittee that no further funding be allocated for the production of any more cyborgs. I think the main thrust of Project Download is too important to channel valuable financial resources to any questionable 'byproducts.' And, quite frankly, I'm not sure that the CIA is the proper agency to administer this project. Your handling of it has certainly left much to be desired. However, we'll take that up during our next session. Right now, unless any of our honored members have any further questions, I think we can adjourn for lunch."

He glanced around the dais, but no one had anything to add.

"Very well, then. On behalf of my fellow members, Mr. Higgins, I'd like to thank you for appearing before this congressional subcommittee and express my appreciation and commend you for your cooperation. You've been extremely helpful, and I can assure you that your views will be given due consideration. This meeting is adjourned until two o'clock this afternoon."

The gavel lifted and the hammer fell.

Dr. Jennifer Stone was waiting for him in the hall outside the meeting room. She was a stunningly attractive woman, in her mid-thirties, with shoulder-length red hair and bright green eyes. Hers was the kind of vivacious beauty that expressed itself no matter how she tried to tone it down, but any man who tried to take her at face value soon found that he had bitten off a lot more than he could chew.

Jennifer Stone had learned at a very early age that beauty such as hers could be as much a liability as an asset. In fact, it could only be an asset if she chose to exploit it, as many attractive women did, but that was not her way. She was too intelligent to downplay her abilities and too proud to be manipulative. Instead, she was aggressive, highly capable and professional to a fault. And until she had met Higgins, she had never been involved with any man. Men, she had found, were much too time consuming. Those who were not intimidated by her strength and her intelligence had a tendency to ask much more of her than she was willing to give. She was married to her career and she had no time for any lovers. So she had held them all at bay with her brisk, professional demeanor and her brook-no-nonsense personality. Until she had met Oliver Higgins. And then something very strange had happened.

Higgins had given her the opportunity of a lifetime. After the tragic murder of Dr. Phillip Gates, the brilliant cybernetics engineer who had headed up the team responsible for Steele and Stalker, Higgins had selected her on the basis of her professional record to come out from Los Alamos, where she was associated with a branch of Project Download, and take over the lab at project headquarters in the Federal Building. She had leaped at the chance to work with Donovan Steele, the first man in history to receive an artificial brain. What she found when she arrived was something even more fascinating.

For the first few days after her arrival, she had thrown herself into the task of supervising the rebuilding of the lab that Stalker had destroyed and trying to recover all the damaged data. She had lived out of her office on the 22nd floor, sleeping on the couch and showering in the basement gym, putting in 18-hour days and driving her staff almost as hard as she drove herself. Higgins had been very much impressed. And she, in turn, had been impressed with him.

He was a handsome man, in his forties, suave and urbane, not at all the sort of dull and officious bureaucrat she had expected. And though he was a layman, the CIA administrator in charge of the project, he had a quick mind and a crisp, professional manner that appealed to her. He never once spoke to her condescendingly, or made a pass, but from the very first had treated her as a colleague, not in the least bit threatened by her intelligence. She was not initially attracted to him, or at least she didn't think she was, but she had summed him up quickly, with a curt mental nod of approval, thinking, "Good. The man's a pro. I can work with him." And then everything went ker-blooey.

He had invited her up to his office one night after she had finished up her day's work at the lab and asked her professional opinion concerning a problem that he wasn't quite sure what to do with. When she had seen what it was, she felt as if she had been gut-punched.

The late Dr. Gates, ever the methodical engineer, had kept a backup copy of Steele's downloaded mental engram matrix in computer storage. Dr. Devon Cooper, the project psychiatrist, whom she had known back at Los Alamos, had pulled a second backup copy of the matrix in order to spend more time analyzing Steele at home. He had felt strongly that Steele, who had a cop's distrust of shrinks, was keeping something back from him, something that was disturbing him profoundly. Gates had given him a VS peripheral that enabled Dev Cooper to speak with the matrix, and the voice synthesizer had been programmed to respond with Steele's own voice. With the assistance of Dr. Julie Nakamura, who had also been killed when Stalker ran amok, Cooper had programmed an imperative into the matrix, roughly an electronic equivalent of truth serum, that was meant to insure that the matrix would respond truthfully to any questions Cooper put to it.

It was that last part that had fascinated Jennifer. An engram matrix was essentially nothing more than software, and software could not "choose" to respond or to respond untruthfully. A computer program did not have free will. It gave the user any data that was requested, provided, of course, that the data was contained within its files. But the engram matrix was a backed-up download of Steele's personality, augmented with ancillary data. It *had* free will. It was *alive*.

Supposedly, it was nothing more than data, software that could not function unless it was loaded into a sophisticated cybernetic brain and brought on line. But they had discovered that the engram matrix was capable of functioning in almost any computer, making that computer "come to life." It was far more than merely software. It was a person without a body. It was human. It was self-aware. And it was an exact duplicate of Steele's personality, an electronic clone.

That discovery had brought Dev Cooper to the edge of a mental breakdown. He had become drug- and alcohol-dependent. He couldn't sleep unless he drank himself into unconsciousness, and he needed to take stimulants to stay awake. Higgins had bugged his apartment and discovered what he had done. While Cooper was away, Higgins had sent agents to his apartment with orders to boot up the matrix so that he could take a download through the phone line, creating yet another backup copy so that he could see what Cooper had been up to. He had believed that Cooper had modified the program in some way, and he had asked Jennifer's expert opinion.

When she made the same discovery that Cooper made, the implications of it had rocked her. Adrenaline trip-hammered through her body as she realized that she had stumbled upon the scientific discovery of the century. And the thrill of the discovery, the staggering significance of it, the stress, the pressure, and all those years of self-denial had opened up the floodgates. It was all released in a torrent of long-repressed sexual energy, and she had practically attacked Higgins, making love with him right there on his office desk.

But in their excitement, they hadn't realized that someone

else was watching: the matrix, still booted up in the computer. And it had switched on the surveillance camera in the office to tape them making love.

What followed had unnerved them both completely. The copy of the matrix still in Cooper's possession had contacted their copy of the matrix through the phone lines and the two had integrated. And then the matrix had utilized the power lines to escape from the computer. It had raided the data banks in the maximum security project lab and there had been nothing they could do to stop it.

And now they had no idea where it was.

Higgins had not dared to give that information to the subcommittee. Carman would have crucified him. Only three people had knowledge of it. Higgins, Stone and Cooper, who was confined to his apartment, under house arrest. There were two agents with him at all times, to make sure that Cooper took no drugs and used no drink. Cooper knew too much for Higgins to risk having him dry out in a hospital. They were doing it the hard way, because they needed him. But unknown to either of them, there was one other person whom Cooper had let in on the secret. Father Liam Casey, the Catholic priest who was Steele's close friend and confessor. And though Cooper wasn't Catholic, he had unburdened his soul to Father Casey in good faith and trust, and it was a trust the worried priest could not betray. Not even Steele knew he had an electronic clone . . . somewhere.

Jennifer Stone took one look at the expression on Higgins' face and didn't need to ask him how it went. It was only a question of hearing the damage report.

"How bad was it?" she asked.

"Bad," said Higgins grimly. "Give me a few minutes, okay? I'm so mad right now, I could shoot that son of a bitch Carman in the head. I need a drink."

He stuck an unlit pipe into his mouth as they headed toward the elevators. A second later, Jennifer heard a sharp snap. He had bitten through the stem. They took the elevator up to the third floor and walked down the long, spacious, carpeted hallway to the congressional lounge that had at one time been the UN delegates' bar. The long bar was at the far end of the large airy lounge, to their right, just past the huge tapestry of the

Great Wall of China that was about the size of a tennis court, a relic from the days of the UN. To their left, the entire wall was glass, affording a view of the rose garden and the East River, with the ruins of the 59th Street Bridge in the background. Low, circular wood tables with luxurious lounge chairs upholstered in black leather were placed around the room. They sat down and Higgins gave the waiter an order for two Scotches, straight up, doubles.

He took the pipe out of his mouth and only then noticed that he had bitten through the stem. He grimaced and put it back in his pocket. Jennifer said nothing. Though she had known him for only a short time, they had become extremely close. They were more than lovers. They were friends and colleagues. And she had never seen him like this before. Except when they made love, Higgins rarely revealed his emotions. Now, the muscles in his neck were corded. His jaw was clenched and his eyes were hard as anthracite. For a long time, he merely stared out the window, without speaking. She gave him time. Their drinks arrived. He tossed his back in two quick swallows and immediately ordered another.

Some legislators and bureaucrats started to drift in to drink their lunch. A few had sat on the committee. They pointedly avoided them. Senator Carman was not among them. Bryce Carman did not drink. Bryce Carman did not smoke. As far as he knew—and being CIA, Higgins knew a *lot*—Bryce Carman didn't even screw. The man seemed to have no vices whatsoever. Unless one counted power. And Carman hoarded power like Midas hoarded gold. Higgins wished to God that he had something on the man, *anything*, but Carman seemed to live up to this nickname—the White Knight. He was pure. And he was a crusader. And he had just reached out with his lance and spiked Higgins to the earth.

"We're dead," said Higgins, finally.

Jennifer merely listened.

"I tried," he continued. "I gave it my best shot. And I really thought I had it working, but that bastard Carman pulled the rug right out from under me. 'On behalf of the committee, I'd like to thank you and commend you for your cooperation. Your views will be given due consideration.' Sanctimonious cocksucker."

Jennifer raised her eyebrows. The language did not offend her, it merely surprised her, coming from Higgins. It could only mean one thing. The worst had happened.

"They cut the funding," she said with a sinking feeling. She had already known it. But somehow, she had hoped that she was wrong.

"Yeah," said Higgins. "Oh, they're going to 'deliberate,' and it looks as if they'll continue to fund the downloading research, but we've built our last cyborg."

"What about Steele?" she said.

Higgins shook his head. "I don't know. They didn't say. I guess we'll have to hope those new upgrades hold up, because there probably won't be anymore. If he breaks now, he'll probably stay broke."

"Surely, they won't just abandon him," she said. "Not after all he's been through?"

"You want to bet?" Higgins smiled wryly. "You know the funny thing about it, though? Steele would probably much rather have it that way. The only thing he hates more than psychiatrists is bureaucrats. He'll go back to the Strike Force once again and be happy as a pig in mud."

"So are we all out of a job?" she asked.

"Not you," said Higgins. "You'll probably be transferred back to Los Alamos. But me, I'm history. Stalker gave Carman the perfect excuse to shut me down. The CIA makes killer cyborgs. So they're scuttling the cyborg project and taking Download away from the agency. And without Download, there's no longer any real reason for the agency to continue to exist. Harding's spineless. He's been sitting on his hands and letting them whittle us away for years. Without Download, we're no longer doing anything the military can't handle. I guess I should start looking for a job."

"You ever think of moving to New Mexico?" she asked.

He raised his eyebrows, then smiled. "You offering to set me up in my own apartment, Doctor? What kind of man do you think I am?"

"The different kind," she said. "The kind who probably wouldn't rattle my chain too much. The kind who'd probably drive any other woman crazy because you don't really need a woman. But then, I don't really need a man. So we're a perfect match."

"Matches start fires."

"Yeah, but we both like the heat."

He smiled. "There is that. Only we're both workaholics. You'd be okay, but what the hell would an ex-spook do in New Mexico? I'm a little old for punching cows."

"Oh, there's lots of things out there for you to punch," she said. "Remember all the times you've told me about your younger days, before you got promoted to a desk? Your eyes always lit up when you spoke about your days out in the field, with that special unit . . . what was it called?"

"The Special Operations Group."

"That's right. Troubleshooters. Hot shots. There's room for hot shots out there, Oliver. It's not like Midtown. The no-man's-land out there is really something. It's *big*. It's wild. You could be young again. There'd be lots out there for a man like you to do. I'm progressive. I don't really mind you having a career so long as you've got your pants down around your ankles when I get home."

"I see. You're only interested in me for sex."

"Isn't that what men are for?"

"Listen to you. Thirty-five years you stayed a virgin and now all of sudden you're a sex maniac."

"I've got a lot of catching up to do. Only I want to do it on my terms, with a man who'll accept me as I am without getting in my hair. Look, we both need a lot of space and we respect that in each other. Neither one of us wants children. We're both aggressive; we're both compulsive. Type-A personalities; we feed off each other's energy and we're great in bed together. So how about it?"

"Is that a marriage proposal, Doctor?"

"*Marriage*?" she said. "Who the hell said anything about marriage? I'm asking you to shack up with me."

"Oh. 'Why buy the cow when you can have the milk for free,' is that it?"

"Yea, cows give manure, too, and it's getting a little deep around here."

"Fuck you."

"Okay. Let's go back to my place. I picked up this new

black leather outfit I've been dying to try out."

He grinned. "You're crazy, you know that?"

"No, just horny," she said. "What do you say? Let's get drunk and fuck our brains out."

"Have you really got a black leather outfit?"

"With matching boots," she said.

"Oooh."

"No, I'll tell you when to say 'oooh.' The girl in the store told me about an interesting game you can play with four sets of handcuffs, a feather and some ice cubes."

*"Ice cubes?"*

"It has to do with timing," she said with a sly smile.

Higgins cleared his throat. "Matching boots, huh?"

"With six-inch heels."

Higgins signaled the waiter.

"Check, please."

On July 4, 1867, General Granville Dodge, chief engineer of the Union Pacific and the man after whom Dodge City was named, chose the site for the east base of the Rockies for the proposed transcontinental railroad. He named the town Cheyenne. The military post established there to protect the railroad workers was named Fort Russell, after a general of the Civil War.

The horse soldiers stationed at Fort Russell played a major part in the expansion of the west. They saw action against the Sioux, led by Sitting Bull and Crazy Horse. They helped put down the Ute uprising. After Wyoming received statehood, the outbreak of the Spanish American War saw infantry troops from Fort Russell fighting in the Philippines. Units from Fort Russell were sent to patrol the Mexican border when Pancho Villa decided to raise a little hell with the United States. And when America entered World War I, Fort Russell played a role as a mobilization and training base for field artillery.

In 1927, the last cavalry units left Fort Russell and three years later, the post was renamed Fort Frances E. Warren, after the Wyoming senator who had won the Congressional Medal of Honor in the Civil War and was the first governor of the state. World War II resulted in dramatic expansion of Fort Warren as a Quartermaster Training Center, and when the Air Force became a separate branch of the service, Fort Warren became an Air Force base, despite the fact it had no runways. It was home to the Aviation Engineer School, later redesignated the USAF Technical School, which grew as various other training departments were transferred in from other bases. But the most significant development in its long history occurred in 1957, when Francis E. Warren became the first operational ICBM base, under the Strategic Air Command.

By 1963, the giant rotary augers mounted on 90-ton cranes had finished excavating the final silo shaft. Upon completion of the complex, Francis E. Warren AFB became the largest missile base in the world, with 20 launch control facilities and 200 silos housing first the Atlas missiles, then the Minuteman ICBMs and, finally, the Peacekeepers. The name had been ill-chosen.

Originally, it had been known as the MX. Its range was 11,000 km. and it carried 10 MIRVed warheads rated at 300 kilotons apiece. The missiles were "cold launched," which meant that instead of allowing the rocket exhaust to flow up past the missile body as it left the silo in what was called a "hot launch," the missile was ejected by means of pressurized gas. Once the missile was clear of the silo, the first stage motor fired. The three main stages of the Peacekeeper were solid-fueled. The fourth and final stage was liquid-fueled, with an axially mounted rocket motor capable of providing velocity changes and eight small engines for attitude control. A self-contained, intertial guidance system was employed, requiring no external inputs once the missile had been launched, although the Peacekeeper was capable of taking updates from the Navstar satellite system.

Prior to its deployment, there had been a great deal of debate concerning how to base the Peacekeeper. Ground deployment was chosen over aircraft, with underground railroad cars in buried tunnels initially favored by the Carter Administration in what was called the Multiple Protective Shelter plan. The Reagan Administration later scrubbed MPS and decided instead to deploy the missiles in existing Minuteman silos until a more suitable long-range option could be settled upon. Deep Underground Basing was proposed, as well as Mobile Basing and Closely Spaced Basing, the theory being that with the missiles "dense-packed," the nuclear explosion of the first incoming enemy warhead would disable those that followed, thereby saving all the missiles from being destroyed in a first strike. At least, that was how it was supposed to work in theory.

And then a science fiction writer by the name of Norman Spinrad wrote a short satirical piece for a publication named *Omni* magazine. In his article, Spinrad mocked the idea of underground railroad tunnels as being a waste of time and money. Why bother tunneling through Nevada like a bunch of moles, he'd written, when a perfectly suitable system of deployment was readily available? Place the missiles in launch-capable railroad cars, he wrote, and attach each one to the tail end of a New York City subway train. You could fire them up through manhole covers. This system of deployment, he argued, tongue-in-cheek, had a great deal to recommend it. For one thing, since the missiles would require military security, a useful byproduct would be troops in New York City's subways, perhaps the only means of rendering the subways safe. And since not even the average New York City commuter knew when the subways ran, it was a cinch the Soviets would have no idea where the missiles were, either. And if even more security was desired, the missile cars could always be shuttled onto the Amtrak system, where they would become lost forever in the twilight zone of train scheduling.

Somebody evidently thought it was a swell idea. A number of special trains were assembled, carrying dummy missiles for test runs throughout the country's rail network. There was nothing to distinguish these dummy missile carriers from any other trains and the idea was to see if anybody noticed them. They didn't. So, on December 19, 1986, the White House announced the President's decision to begin development on a rail garrison system for the Peacekeeper ICBM. The proposed system would initially consist of 50 Peacekeeper missiles deployed on 25 Air Force trains with two missiles per train. Each train would include two locomotives, two security cars, two missile launch cars, one launch control car and one maintenance car. The security cars would contain equipment for security control and monitoring, plus a security force to protect the missile. Each launch car would house the missile itself and provide a launch platform. The launch control car would contain the command control equipment necessary for targeting and launch operations, and the maintenance car would hold spare parts and components. The trains would be based in secure garrisons on existing Air Force Bases throughout the country, with four to six trains parked in "train alert shelters" during normal day-to-day operations with the missiles on continuous strategic alert. And if things started to get tense, the "peace trains" would all pull out and disperse throughout the nation's railway system. And Warren was designated as the main operating base.

The first Peacekeepers were installed in existing Minuteman silos until the new deployment system could be made operational. The silos were updated with better control, shock absorption and communications systems. The W-87 warheads were designed to effectively destroy the "super-hardened" Soviet missile silos and leadership bunkers. Each silo had a fenced-off surface area of two acres that was monitored by ground sensors. The silos were 100 feet deep and covered with a roughly hexagonal-shaped hatch weighing 110 tons. A cable-actuated system was capable of opening the missile hatch a few inches at a time along a short single track for maintenance purposes, but in the event of a launch, huge pistons "popped" the heavy hatch as if it were a 110-ton champagne cork.

In order to gain access to the silo, it was necessary to open a round black hatch by means of four separate combination locks, two in the adjoining security hatch and two in the access hatch itself. Once that was accomplished, it was necessary to wait about a half an hour for the 7-ton steel plug covering the access hatch to retract upon a giant screw. When the plug reached the bottom, the missile maintenance crew could then climb down the ladder in the narrow access tube.

Each Launch Control Facility was on a similar plot, with access to the Launch Control Capsule gained through the LCF Building on the surface. To get down inside "the hole," which was anywhere from 60 to 100 feet below the surface, depending on the geology of the site, it was necessary to pass a security checkpoint topside manned by well-trained guards, then descend in an elevator and go through two massive, hermetically sealed, eight-foot-wide steel doors. The LCC itself was gimbaled and hydraulically balanced, manned by a missile combat crew commander and a deputy missile combat crew commander. Some were male, some were female. All were young, with a median age of around 24. They wore blue uniforms with colored silk scarves and they were armed with .38 caliber revolvers.

Each crew served a 24-hour tour known as an "alert." It was monotonous duty. Each underground LCC was about the size of a small mobile home, packed with monitoring and communications equipment, and the control room itself was about 6 feet by 25 feet. The targets of each missile were already programmed into its on-board computer, which could retain a hundred targets simultaneously. The launch control team could change the targeting kits as ordered by CINCSAC, out of Offut Air Force Base. Otherwise, they studied their technical orders, decoded routine alerts and ran checks on the missiles under their control. That still left them with a lot of time on their hands.

To keep from getting bored, they made phone calls to family or friends, played games, read books, listened to the radio or watched TV. Occasionally, some animal like a jack rabbit— or some pain-in-the-ass throwing rocks over the fence into the compound—would set off a ground sensor and trigger an alarm. Otherwise, there wasn't much to do. A lot of crews studied for degrees. They were also regularly evaluated by psychiatrists, though there were many redundancies built into the system to secure against an unauthorized launch.

The two crew commanders sat in track-mounted chairs equipped with seat belts, at right angles to each other, separated by about 15 feet. It was necessary for both of them to turn their keys at the same time and hold them for two seconds. The distance between them rendered it impossible for one of them to freak out, overpower the other, and turn both keys to initiate the launch sequence. And even if the impossible were somehow to happen, it took *two* separate Launch Control Facilities to effect a launch.

The first warning would come as an oscillating note over the loudspeaker that signified the order to seal up and go to emergency air. The crew would then each open one of the two locks on a red safe that contained their orders and their keys. Each of them had memorized one combination that was unknown to the other. A printed code would appear on a panel before them. They then checked the launch code in their orders against the one they had received. If they matched, the launch command was valid. Each missileer then entered his or her individual code, unknown to his or her partner, to gain access to the firing circuits. They turned their keys simultaneously and held them for two seconds, following a well-practiced procedure and calling out the steps. If one of them were to hesitate, the other was under orders to draw his or her weapon and enforce immediate compliance. The point of this procedure was somewhat debateable, since if one of the missileers was forced to shoot the other, the launch could not take place, but apparently it was felt that the psychological factor of having a pistol pointed at a hesitating missileer would serve its purpose. In any case, once the birds were launched, the odds were that the missileers would die.

Ground-based missiles were vulnerable to enemy attack. If an enemy warhead struck, the missile crews would not survive. Both the Soviet Union and the United States knew where each other's missiles were within a matter of inches, thanks to satellite surveillance. The whole system was based upon deterrence. If the Soviets were to launch their missiles, the US could go to DEFCON 1 and counterattack with all its missiles as soon as the enemy launch signatures were detected. They'd get us, but we'd also get them. The acronym for this eye-for-an-eye strategy was ironically appropriate—MAD, which stood for "Mutually Assured Destruction."

Needless to say, no one was very comfortable with this MAD idea. As the fictional launch control computer stated in the movie *WarGames*, the only way to win was not to play. But then, winning was always a part of human nature. There had to be a way to win this game.

Okay then, said the strategists in the Pentagon, forget MAD. It's an awkward-sounding acronym anyway. Let's talk "Counterforce." Target the enemy's weapons. Of course, they had satellites too, and they would do the same to ours, at least until we all started putting our bombs aboard Orange Blossom Specials. But maybe we could shoot their missiles down before they got to us, with ABMs or laser beams or death rays deployed on satellites in outer space. So the debates went on, new plans were made, the wargamers played their "simulations," the missile crews went through their drills and the high-stakes game of bluff poker went on with no one daring to lay down their cards. Until the day came when the clock finally ran out. And the game ran into Sudden Death.

Sgt. Reese Tracy stood grabbing a quick smoke by his jeep on the windswept plain outside Cheyenne. A few feet away from him was a fenced enclosure that contained one of the missile Launch Control Facilities. It didn't look like much. Only the dilapidated LCF Building, surrounded by sagebrush. It reminded him of a tumble-down building in a ghost town. In fact, it *did* have ghosts. Two missileers were buried here, 60 feet below the ground, sealed up as if inside a mausoleum. And the detail he was in charge of was in the process of trying to open up that mausoleum using heavy equipment. It was a slow, laborious process.

Tracy nervously lit up another cigarette. It felt strange being out here. It gave him chills. There was a large area to the southeast that was still hot. They were uncomfortably close to it. Earlier in the day, they had examined a silo from which a Peacekeeper missile had been fired. The hatch had been popped open, thrown for a distance of almost a quarter mile. Birds were nesting in the empty, dust-filled shaft. But there were still other silos from which the missiles hadn't been fired. And Tracy was part of a unit that was taking inventory.

He tried to imagine what it had been like. People dying by the thousands. By the millions. Dropping like flies as the virus had spread with devastating speed throughout the world, worse than any fallout. The missile crews had sat down in their Launch Control Capsules, listening to radios or watching it on television. They would have heard the radio stations falling silent. They would have heard or seen the broadcasters dying on the air. The launch order had come down. The official line was that the Russians had launched first, but no one was really sure. At this point, it didn't really make much difference. The birds had flown, but most of them had never gotten off the ground. Otherwise, thought Tracy, there probably wouldn't *be* any ground for him to stand on. The world's suicide attempt had been a failed one. The planet had been badly wounded, but she had survived. Just barely. And now....

Tracy wasn't sure about what they were doing now. His unit had moved in to Francis E. Warren about a month ago, coming up from Denver to join the squadron led by General Zachary Cord. General Cord was the law in this part of the country, which was mostly large stretches of desolate no-man's-land. The units he had brought together at the old Warren Air Force Base were among the finest fighting troops in the entire military. He had gathered together men from surviving units of the Delta Force and Rangers and incorporated them into his own special elite unit, Cobra Force.

That name had been made legend by the Army's most famous living general. They were the elite of the elite, grown up out of a small assault team that Cord was in command of in his younger days as a captain, a unit of the CIA's Special Operations Group. Their skill was such that they seemed almost supernatural, and all the other units in the military regarded them with awe. They wore distinctive uniforms, dark forest green trimmed with black, and their shoulders and black berets bore the Cobra Force patch, a black, hooded snake with jaws agape over crossed yellow lightning bolts on a scarlet background.

Their specialty was "pacification." They were the most decorated soldiers of the old Special Operations Group. When the SOG had been officially disbanded, Cord, then a colonel, had been allowed to retain his own unit. He was given authority to expand the Cobra Force as a tactical troubleshooter force to take over the functions of the SOG, only this time under the command of the Army rather than the CIA, which had been relegated to a largely bureaucratic function. Since that time, the exploits of the Cobra Force had grown to almost mythic proportions.

They had fought and defeated bands of savage raiders all across the country. They had stormed outlaw enclaves, fought renegade National Guard and police units. Their training program, organized by Cord himself, was rigorous enough to kill some of those who failed to measure up, and those who managed to make the grade knew that they were part of something very special indeed. And Cord made sure that they were treated special. They were like the Praetorians of Rome, the legendary Immortals of ancient Persia, the ninjas of Japan. They answered to nobody but Cord. About the most a senior officer from any other unit could expect from them was a salute. Tracy was impressed with them, but they also made him nervous.

Since moving into the old, deserted base, Cord had put the other units under his command to work on refurbishment and reconstruction. The troops were quartered in brick barracks and the senior officers lived in the old, colonial-style brick homes that dated back to the early days of the 20th Century. Cord himself lived in an elegant brick mansion with a columned portico, wood floors and a grand staircase with teak railings. A lifelong bachelor, Cord had surrounded himself with comfort. He had orderlies and servants to see to his every need, and he often threw elegant dinners for his men in the style of old frontier post commanders. He even held military balls. He had brought order back to this part of the country, and the town of Cheyenne had swelled with people moving in from outlying settlements. But Tracy had his doubts about what they were doing here.

A lot of the missile silos throughout the country had been destroyed by Soviet strikes during the war, and many were located in hot spots that were still unsafe to enter. But there were still silos at Warren that were occupied by Peacekeepers and a few leftover Minuteman missiles. The Rail Garrison Plan, delayed time and again by various bureaucratic snafus, had only started to be implemented when the shit had hit the fan. Warren had only three missile trains standing in their garrisons, which was as far as the new deployment plan had come. And there were the underground LCCs, such as the one they were engaged in opening, that had received the order to launch, but had never been able to carry it out. Before they had sealed up, the airborne virus got to them and killed the launch crews, leaving the missiles standing in launch mode, like the world's biggest cocked and loaded guns.

Tracy had first thought their purpose here was to deactivate those missiles, but they had opened up several silos so far and they hadn't dismantled a single one. In fact, at those silos they had already opened, there were maintenance crews at work, checking out the systems and replacing components. And there were crews at work upon the trains.

*For what?*

Assigned to every one of those crews, as to his own detail, were commandos of the Cobra Force. Scuttlebutt among those units recently arrived had Cord spending most of his time down in the main launch control center, conferring with the civilian scientists sent out by the federal authorities from back east. Only no one ever saw much of those scientists. No one ever spoke to them. They were quartered in one of the large brick mansions around the circular, tree-lined drive where the senior officers lived, and that mansion was guarded around the clock by members of the Cobra Force.

Sgt. Tracy had a horrible suspicion that their purpose here at Warren was not to deactivate the missiles at all, but to bring them back on line. In fact, they had never gone *off* line. The question was, after all these years, were they still operational? Tracy's orders were to report precisely the condition of every silo that they opened up, especially the LCCs. How far had the crews inside gotten in their launch procedures before they had died? Had they opened up the red safe that contained their orders? Had they confirmed the launch codes? Had they accessed the firing mechanisms? Tracy was supposed to report everything they found inside down to the last detail. They were not to touch anything. They were not to remove the bodies. They were simply to open up the silos and the Launch Control Capsules, observe in detail and report.

Corporal Pat Summers came trotting up to his jeep.

"We've got it open," she said, slightly out of breath. "Want to see?"

"No," said Tracy, tightly. "Not really."

She grimaced. "Yeah, I know what you mean. Got a cigarette?"

He passed her the pack. Most of the soldiers smoked. It was one of their few privileges. Cigarettes made from the tobacco grown in the southern agro-communes were ludicrously expensive due to taxes, but soldiers got them cheap. It settled nerves and helped suppress the appetite, which was no small thing, because of the chronic shortages.

"I hate this part," said Tracy.

"Me, too," she said. "God, the first one we broke into, I was scared shitless. I know they told us the virus wouldn't still be active after all this time, but still.... It doesn't seem to bother the Cobras, though."

"Nothing bothers them," said Tracy. "They're fucking machines."

"They give me the creeps," said Summers. "I've had several of them make passes at me. Cord doesn't allow women in Cobra Force, so they're all a bunch of horny motherfuckers. But they can whack off or screw the townies, for all I care. I wouldn't want to be caught alone with any of 'em. Snaky bastards." She grinned at her unintentional pun. "Snaky Cobras. That's a good one, huh?"

"Patty, what do you think about all this?" asked Tracy.

She gave him a sharp glance. They'd all been having the same thoughts, but so far, none of them had spoken them out loud.

"Shit, Trace, I don't know," she said. "It's all sorta spooky, ain't it?"

"You want to know what I think?"

"What?" she said with forced nonchalance.

"I don't think our job here is to disarm any of those missiles," he said. "I think it's all a smoke screen."

"You, too, huh?"

"Yeah." He took a deep breath and let it out slowly. "I think Cord wants to get those birds operational."

She was silent for a moment. "Why would he want to do that? You figure he knows something we don't?"

"Maybe. Nobody ever tells us anything. We have no need to know," he added wryly.

"We've still got missiles," she said. "It stands to reason the Russians probably do, too. You think maybe they found out the Russians are trying to finish what they started?"

"Or maybe we are," he replied.

"I don't believe that."

"Why not? Nobody really knows who pushed the button first."

"Someone's got to know."

"Well, if they do, they're not telling us, that's for sure," said Tracy. "Those civilian scientists are always kept under guard. Why?"

"It's for their own protection."

"Against whom? *Us*?"

"Well, they're important personnel...."

"They're practically prisoners," said Tracy. "I don't know anybody who's actually talked to any of them. Do you?"

"What are you saying?"

"Hell, I'm not sure what I'm saying," he replied. "I only know there's something weird going on. If we're not going to use these missiles, why aren't we dismantling them?"

"Well, for defense...."

"Against what?" said Tracy. "A Soviet attack? You really believe that? They're probably in even worse shape than we are."

"Well, we don't really know what's happening over there. They could be in a lot worse shape than we are. Or maybe—"

"Or maybe we want to make *sure* they are," said Tracy. "Jesus, I don't like what I'm thinking, Pat. These things scare the shit out of me. We oughta be taking them apart. Instead, we've got maintenance crews in all the silos and the LCCs we've opened up. What the hell for? Haven't we learned anything, for God's sakes?"

She did not respond.

"I don't know what the hell we're doing," Tracy said. "Just like those two poor bastards down there didn't know what they were doing. A bunch of greasy terrorists released the goddamn plague, and we thought the Russians did it; they thought we did it, and between us, we almost blew up the fucking world. We oughta be melting them down into scrap metal. Only we're not doing that. So what the hell *are* we doing?"

"You better lower your voice," she said.

Some of the people were coming out of the Launch Control Facility.

"Is it just me?" Tracy said. "Doesn't it bother you?"

"Yeah," she said softly. "It bothers me. But what difference does that make? I don't see what we can do about it."

"They can't be thinking of starting the whole thing up again," said Tracy. "They just *can't* be. It's fucking *insane*."

One of the Cobras was beckoning to Tracy. Time to go down and make out his report.

"Jesus." Tracy threw down his cigarette butt. "What are we doing? What the *hell* are we doing?"

Pat Summers followed him as he went through the gate and headed over to the LCF. The three Cobras were waiting for them.

"You ready to go down, Sergeant, or are you still goldbricking?" one of them said.

"All right, all right, let's do it," Tracy replied irritably. He had his clipboard out, ready to take notes on what they found.

They went inside the LCF building. It was shaped like a rectangle, covered with tan-colored aluminum siding, with a garage. In the days before the war, the personnel who were assigned here worked a three-day shift, living three days on the site with three to six days off. From Warren, the closest LCF was about 35 miles to the north and the farthest, known to the base personnel as "Hotel," was about 150 miles to the east. The soldiers would drive out to the LCFs in Chevy or Dodge vans that would then take the personnel coming off duty back to the base. The last shift was still here.

As they went through the door, they entered a short entry hall with an open closet to the left. To the right was the flight security controller's office, the nerve center for the security police. It was walled off, with a window looking in. The door of the small office had been busted in. There were two bodies inside, badly decomposed, one seated in a chair, the other sprawled out on the floor in front of the lockers. There were windows on three sides of the office, looking out at the barren expanse of desert. Tracy noted the positions of the bodies, then continued on into the building.

They entered the large carpeted main room that held couches, a color TV, chairs and a pool table. There was a dining area and counters holding coffee makers, sugar, creamer, and various utensils. There was a Coke machine, magazines, a VCR and shelves containing books and video cassettes. Tracy pulled one of the cassettes off the shelf and read the label.

"*Apocalypse Now.*"

He glanced at Pat. She compressed her lips and shook her head.

The bodies of two security policemen were on the floor, nothing left of them but bones. The kitchen was in the back, to the left, through a swinging door. It had a grill, a refrigerator, ovens and a large freezer. They found what was left of the cook, sprawled on the floor in front of the open refrigerator door. In the back were two bathrooms, one for men and one for women. The men's room was empty. The women's room held one corpse, an SP. She was kneeling, draped over the toilet. She died in the act of throwing up blood. They found the rest of the bodies in the bunkrooms. There was a faded old rock and roll poster on the wall, bearing the legend "Metallica" and depicting a grinning death's head. Tracy swallowed hard and turned away.

"Okay," he said. "Let's go down in the hole."

They went back into the flight security controller's office. Behind the desk was a metal door with a window in the middle and a wall phone beside it, a direct line down to the crew. The door had been forced open. They entered the elevator. Power had been restored to the facility by the diesel-fueled generators. They got into the elevator and started to descend.

The elevator was an open, wire cage. The walls of the shaft were bright yellow as they descended. When they got to the bottom, everything was gray. They stepped out into a little room. There was a heavy blast door directly in front of them, bearing the SAC emblem. To the right, in a recessed area, was a ladder in an access tube. There was a giant handle on the door, operated by a crank. It had been opened, giving access to the capsule junction. Through the door and to the left was the launch control equipment area, which held a brine chiller, the diesel generator, one month's supply of diesel fuel, air tubes with filters—part of the recycling system—and barrels with water and food for 30 days. The service had acronyms for everything. The MREs (Meals Ready to Eat) were stored in green plastic packets with foil on the inside. They were to be mixed with boiled water.

Access to the LCC itself was on the right, through a concrete and steel door that weighed three and half tons. It was meant to be opened from the inside. Breaking into it had taken most of the day. Once through it, they entered a square tunnel about four feet tall and six feet long. They crawled through into the capsule. It was a dark accoustical enclosure painted gray. The Boeing computer racks were ancient, dating back to the 60s. It looked like a set from an old science fiction movie, all wires, vacuum tubes and dials. When the cooling system was operating, the crews could have felt the air gushing around the racks. The computers had long since overheated, but Tracy knew that after he was finished here, the maintenance crews would start replacing them. Purely as a precaution, of course, to run checks on the systems and the missile before it was dismantled. Sure, he thought.

There was a small bed with a brown army blanket on it, a toilet, a sink, and a shower, with a curtain for privacy. There was also a toaster oven, a small refrigerator that held cans of soda pop, a color television set, and one of the missileers had brought down a portable radio, what they used to call a "boom box." There were several tape cassettes beside it. Tracy punched the eject button and removed the cassette from the tape deck. Guns n' Roses. The cassette was titled "Appetite for Destruction."

The corpses of the two missileers were strapped into their chairs. Skeletons in blue uniforms, with yellow scarves around their necks. By the scraggly remains of hair, they could tell that both were women. Tracy tried not to look at their name tags. He didn't want to know their names. They had opened up the safe and removed their orders and their keys. Both keys had been inserted and turned, allowing access to the firing mechanisms. And then they died, both with their heads back, jaws agape in never-ending silent screams.

One of them had propped a photograph on the console before her. Tracy picked it up. It showed two people in late middle age, a man and a woman, both smiling, with their arms around each other. The inscription read, "Make us proud, honey. Love, Mom and Dad."

"Come on, Sergeant, get a move on," one of the Cobras said. "We haven't got all day."

"Yeah, sure," said Tracy. He bit his lower lip and started making out his report.

• • •

As she went down the hall to the elevator banks, Raven Scarpetti was followed closely by three security guards who watched her walk appreciatively. They undressed her with their eyes. It didn't bother her. She was used to that kind of reaction from most men. And the way she walked tended to provoke it.

Women who deliberately tried to walk in a sexually provocative manner often weren't able to pull it off without making it look exaggerated and artificial, because it was not their natural way of walking. But hookers were experts at it, largely because it *became* natural for them. They did it without thinking. And Raven didn't bother trying to change the way she walked simply because she was no longer turning tricks.

She didn't bother trying to change the way she talked or the way she dressed either. She wasn't particularly proud of her former occupation. Far from it. But it was a part of who she was and she wasn't about to erase that aspect of her life. It had happened and she was not going to deny it. She had been a teenaged girl when her crime boss boyfriend had dumped her on a sadistic pimp who brutalized her, and she had grown up in "the life." It had forged her, hardened her and given her instincts for survival that had served her well. She wore her past life as a badge of defiance, as if to say, "That's right, I was a hooker. Want to make something of it?" It was like a veteran's battle scar. She wouldn't think of trying to remove it. It was something she had fought and lived through. And if her man could accept her as she was, then that was good enough for her and anybody else could go to hell.

The doors slid shut and the elevator started to descend. She felt the guards' eyes on her. Her breasts were on the small side, so men had a tendency to focus on her long and well-shaped legs. She knew they were outstanding legs, her best feature, aside from her face, which made her look younger than she really was. In her early twenties, she looked not a day over eighteen. She was pretty, but that prettiness was touched with feral hardness, a trashy combination few men could resist. She caught them staring at her legs and they quickly looked away.

"Like what you see?" she asked.

The guards exchanged glances and one of them cleared his

throat. "Sorry, ma'am. Didn't mean to stare."

"Bullshit."

The man grimaced uncomfortably. "Yes, ma'am."

She smiled. The elevator stopped in the basement and they transferred to another one that took them down to the maximum security levels. It descended to B-3. The doors opened on what looked like a concrete bunker. Two helmeted soldiers in combat fatigues, armed with automatic weapons, stood before them. They left the elevator and turned down a short corridor that led to a security post. Beside it, behind a gate, was a massive, barred steel door. There were two other soldiers stationed on either side of it and another sat behind a console.

"Ms. Raven Scarpetti to see Lieutenant Steele," said one of the guards.

"Morning, ma'am," said the man behind the console. He checked her pass. "Thank you, ma'am. Step through the gate, please."

She went through the gate, which scanned her as she passed through it. It didn't pick up any weapons. She had left the snubnosed .38 Smith and Wesson Airweight she kept in her purse at the security post up in the lobby. The man at the console spoke into his mike to another security post behind the heavy door. It was opened electronically from inside.

They passed through and went down a corridor that ended at the entrance to the project lab. Another two soldiers were posted at the doors. After entering the lab complex, they made their way past banks of electronic equipment and computers, desk terminals and office cubicles manned by busy personnel and passed through another door at the back of the complex. This door opened onto a short, carpeted corridor. There were several doors leading into rooms on either side. They stopped at the third one on their left and one of the guards knocked.

"Come in," said a voice from inside.

The guard opened the door and stood aside to let Raven enter. Inside, it was about the size of an average hotel room. And it looked like an average hotel room, too. The only real difference was the lack of windows. There was dark carpet on the floor, the better to conceal stains; a queen-sized bed; a reading chair with a standing lamp beside it; a round table with two straight-backed chairs pushed up to it; a bureau opposite the bed with a television set on top of it; a small sound system; a bathroom to the left of the entryway and a walk-in closet. There were several non-descript prints hanging on the wall, a lamp on the bureau beside the television and two light fixtures bolted to the wall on either side of the bed, above the nightstands. It was reasonably comfortable, but hardly homey.

Donovan Steele stretched out on the bed, dressed only in a robe, reading a book. An old science fiction novel by William Gibson. He looked up, smiled and put the book down on the bed as Raven came in and shut the door behind her. There was a stack of novels piled on the nightstand to his right.

"So," she said, "read any good books lately?"

"Not many, but this one's not half bad," said Steele. "This guy was writing about people wired up and interfacing with computers long before they ever came up with the biochip. They called it 'cyberpunk,' according to the jacket copy."

"*Cyberpunk*?" she said.

"Yeah. Chips and drugs and rock n' roll. Strong stuff. It's interesting how close he came, in some ways. Must've been a strange young man."

She sat down beside him on the bed and glanced at the author's photo on the book jacket. "Looks like a hip undertaker," she said. "Kinda cute, though."

"And here I thought you went for the macho type," he said.

"Nah, they're a pain in the ass. Like you." She took his hand. "I miss you, lover."

"I miss you, too."

She leaned forward and kissed him. He put his arms around her, nysteel arms covered with polymer skin, arms that could so easily crush her. They held the kiss for a long time, her tongue slipping into his mouth, eagerly seeking his, her hands entwined in his dark hair. He slipped his hand under her dress. She wasn't wearing panties. He caressed her softly, knowing that to her it felt like a perfectly normal human hand, but to him, it wasn't quite the same.

On close examination, it looked like an ordinary hand of flesh and blood, but there was a small indentation in the palm, sheathed with polymer skin. It resembled a scar, except that it was perfectly round, like a quarter. Initially, it had been a gunport for a sophisticated dart launcher built into his left forearm, but since his last trip to "the body shop," as he referred to it, his systems had been upgraded. The entire left arm, which had sustained damage in his fight with Stalker, had been removed and replaced with a much more sophisticated prosthesis that now contained a built-in carbon dioxide laser slaved to his cybernetic brain.

It was more than a little unsettling for him to think that he was caressing her with such an awesome weapon, but it was more than that. It was a part of him, as much as his flesh and blood parts were, and with the laser tube retracted into his forearm, there was no danger to her. The tiny sensors in his polymer skin transmitted information to his cybernetic brain, where it was translated into "feeling," a sense of touch that could be either normal or far more acute than normal, depending on how he adjusted the sensitivity.

As he touched her, he turned his sensors up all the way and his mind filled with the warmth and softness of her. If an ordinary man could have experienced such intensity of feeling, it would have been more than enough to make him climax on the spot, but Steele was not an ordinary man. His cybernetic brain gave him more complete control of his organic functions that any ordinary man could possibly achieve. As he made love to her with that part of him that was still flesh and blood, the sensors built into his nysteel prosthetics flooded him with the taut and silky feel of her and his computer brain allowed him to exert a measure of control that ordinary men could only dream of.

Three and a half hours later, Raven lay beside him, filmed with a sheen of sweat, her short black hair hanging down into her eyes as she gently stroked his chest.

"God, no one ever loved me the way you do," she murmured dreamily.

"Yeah, cyborgs make the ultimate sex toys."

She grimaced. "Don't. It isn't just the sex and you know it. Don't get me wrong, the sex is incredible, but there's a lot more to it than that. I've had my share of studs, but none of them have ever made me feel as *wanted* as you do." She sighed. "I wish to hell you'd lighten up and stop laying all these guilt trips on yourself. If I can accept you the way you are, why can't you?"

"Maybe I just don't accept things as easily as you do," he said. "Don't get me wrong, that's not a criticism. I envy you for it."

"You think I'd love you any less the way you were before?"

"It isn't that," he said. "It's like I told you, it isn't you. It's me."

"What is it, Steele? How can I help?"

"I don't know if you can." He stared up at the ceiling. "Just now, when we were making love, I had this brief flash . . . like a fragment of a memory. . . ."

"What was it?"

He sighed and looked at her. "It's probably not the most flattering thing to say, but while we were making love, for a moment, just an instant, I had this fleeting image of someone else . . . but I don't know who she was. I have these . . . gaps. I can't account for them."

"Was she blonde and very beautiful?" said Raven after a moment's hesitation.

He frowned. "Yes. How did you know?"

She signed. "It was your ex-wife."

He stared at her. "My ex-wife? I was *married*?"

She nodded.

"Jesus, I don't even remember."

"They said I shouldn't talk about it. They've probably got this room bugged, but fuck it, I don't care. What they did was wrong. It stinks. And I'm not gonna be a part of it."

"What are you talking about?"

"They told you that you're being kept here until they can make sure all the new upgrades work properly," she said, "but there's more to it than that. They modified your engram matrix. They went in and erased some things. That's why you have those gaps. It isn't because there's anything wrong with you. They did it. Higgins and that Dr. Stone."

"Tell me," he said, frowning.

"You were married. For almost twenty years."

*"Twenty years?"*

"Her name was Janice. I met her once, after she divorced you. She was about your age, very beautiful and very classy. But she wasn't very nice." Raven grimaced. "Well, that's probably not fair. I guess I'm prejudiced. She hurt you. I didn't like her very much and she sure as hell didn't like me. She looked at me like I was trash. And I guess from her point of view, I am."

"I can't remember anything about her," Steele said, stunned. "Just that fleeting image of her face.... Did we ... were there any children?"

"You had two kids. Your son, Jason, and your daughter, Cory."

"Jesus Christ."

"You don't remember any of this, do you?"

He shook his head with disbelief.

"From what you told me, your marriage was pretty rocky for a long time. After you were shot and they put you back together as a cyborg, your wife divorced you because she couldn't handle it. She—"

The door suddenly flew open and three security guards burst in.

"I'm sorry, Miss Scarpetti, you're going to have to leave. Right now."

"She's not going anywhere," said Steele, sitting up in bed. There was a hard edge to his voice. "Get the hell out of here."

"I'm sorry, Lieutenant, we can't do that," said the guard. "Please. This isn't anything personal, sir. I don't like doing this, but we've got our orders."

Steele's eyes suddenly started to glow. The pupils became brightly illuminated with red light as his laser designator system switched in. He had no intention of shooting at these men, but his eyes had a tendency to light up whenever he got angry. It had a very unsettling effect on people. It had that effect on the guards.

"Get out," he said.

"Please, sir ... don't make this difficult for us."

"If you intend to take her out of here, you'll have to go through me," he said.

"That won't be necessary," said Jennifer Stone from behind the guards. She came into the room. "Please excuse the intrusion. We'll give you some time to get dressed. Then I'll come back in and we can discuss this reasonably."

"She's not leaving," Steele said.

"As you wish. Gentlemen, let's give these people some privacy."

They left and closed the door behind them.

"I'd better get dressed," said Raven, getting out of bed. "I shouldn't have said anything. I should've waited till you'd been released."

"So that's why I've been kept here," Steele said. "They did a little washing on my brain and they wanted to see if it would take."

"I should've kept my mouth shut," she said. "I guess I've really screwed things up."

"I'm glad you told me." Steele got up and went over to the closet. He started putting on his clothes. "I'm getting out of here."

"They may not want to let you leave yet."

"Then they're going to have to stop me," Steele said. "But one thing's for sure. I'm not leaving till I get some answers."

# 3

"We never had any intention of keeping it from you," said Dr. Stone. "Even if we had, a moment's thought would tell you that it would have been impossible. You're a public figure, Steele. What happened when you fought Stalker was given wide coverage in the media. They knew about your daughter's involvement, and they knew how she died, caught in the crossfire of the battle. Aside from that, you have friends, your fellow officers on the Strike Force, many of whom have known you and your family for years. There's no way we could have kept it secret from you, even if we'd wanted to."

"Then . . . *why*, for God's sake?" asked Steele.

"You were severely traumatized," she said. "Your daughter was killed before your very eyes. And Stalker had once been your partner and close friend, Officer Mick Taylor. Aside from the extensive physical damage you sustained in your fight with him, there was profound emotional damage as well. And you were experiencing other problems, problems that you had tried to keep from us. I'm referring to the fact that the ancillary engram data used to supplement your matrix had started to express itself through your subconscious. You were having dreams about past lives and experiences that you could not account for. We call them fragments of 'ghost personalities.' You should have told us about it immediately, yet you kept it to yourself."

"How did you know?" Steele asked.

"We have Dr. Cooper to thank for that. Exactly how we found out about it is immaterial at the moment, but the important fact is that you were in trouble and you didn't tell us. You were afraid we'd put you on downtime to debug your engram matrix, and you thought that when you came out of it again, you might not be the same."

"Yeah," said Steele, slowly, still trying to figure out how they could have known. He knew that Raven never would have told them, and he'd been sure there were no bugs in his apartment, but apparently, he had been wrong. How else could they have known?

"Do you feel any different?"

"There's a lot I can't remember. It's like I've got amnesia. . . ."

"But do you *feel* any different? Do you feel changed in any way?"

"Jesus, how the hell would I *know*?"

"I'll show you," she said. "Who's Jake Hardesty?"

"Chief of Strike Force."

"Liam Casey?"

"Father Casey. My old friend, the priest from St. Vincent's—"

"You have a .45 Colt semiautomatic. What special significance does it have?"

"It was my father's. . . . Jesus, I *do* remember!"

"Of course you do," she said. "We didn't remove *all* your memories. We only removed certain specific ones. Now, tell me about your ex-wife. What was she like?"

"I. . . ." He shook his head, mystified. "I have no idea. I know she was a blonde, but. . . ."

"Tell me about your daughter, Cory."

"She's dead."

"Yes, you know that now, but what was she like?"

He stared at her.

"How old was she?"

Steele moistened his lips. He was drawing a complete blank.

"What color hair did she have? What color eyes?"

"*Stop it*!" Raven shouted. "Jesus fucking Christ! What are you trying to *do* to him?"

"I'm trying to prove a point, Miss Scarpetti. I'd hoped to do this another way, but I'm afraid you've forced the issue." She looked at Steele. "While you were down for repairs and upgrading, we accessed your engram matrix and ran a program to isolate all memories you had of Stalker or Mick Taylor, your ex-wife, your son and your daughter. Then we ran a download to pull those specific engrams. Nothing else. You're still essentially the same man you always were, only you don't remember being married and you have no memories of your family. Now the point is that we can give you back those memories at any time. All it requires is a loading procedure. The reason why we did it in the first place is that you were severely traumatized by the death of your daughter and your final encounter with Stalker. You were also severely damaged physically. It required extensive reconstruction. We wanted to make sure that you were fully functional, and we didn't want your recuperation complicated by emotional trauma. So we removed the sources of that trauma."

"Just like that," said Steele. "You simply wiped out twenty years of my life, just like that."

"Not all twenty years," she said, "just certain segments of it. That explains those gaps you have. We wanted to prove to you that we could make changes in your engram matrix without causing any significant changes in your personality or loss of identity. We didn't try to keep any of it a secret. Miss Scarpetti was fully briefed about it, and I was under the impression that she understood. She was given special clearance to visit you here on the condition that she would follow procedure and give us her full cooperation. Under the circumstances, it will now be necessary to revoke her clearance. However, as a result of recent developments, the point is really moot, in any case."

"What do you mean?" asked Steele.

"Well, you may as well know now. The project has been scrubbed. The committee has decided to cut our funding. We don't yet know for sure, but at this point, it seems probable that the Download Project will be transferred to Los Alamos. The agency will no longer have control of it. In fact, there may not even be an agency after this. Higgins seems to think that Senator Carman will take advantage of this opportunity to disband the CIA. If that happens, most of the agency personnel will probably be transferred to the military or to other existing departments."

"What about me?" asked Steele.

"I can't really answer that," she said. "At this point, I simply don't know. Higgins seems to think that they'll just cut you loose and you'll be free to go back to Strike Force. However, they might have other plans for you. Right now, we just don't know."

"I see," said Steele. "Well, that's not the worst news I've ever heard."

"You realize that once the project is officially shut down, unless they make some sort of separate determination in your case, you'll be completely on your own. You won't have any more support. If you experience any problems after that, we won't be here to help you."

"I managed just fine before you people came along and turned my whole life upside down," said Steele. "I never asked for this. And I never expected any guarantees. It might be nice to get back to Strike Force and live a normal live for a change. Or as normal a life as a cyborg can hope for, anyway."

Jennifer smiled. "Higgins predicted you'd react that way."

"Did he?" Steele said. "Well, I'll have a few things to say to him before we call it quits, but before I leave here, you're going to give me back what you took from me. You had no right to do that, Doctor. No goddamn right at all. I may have lost my family, but I'll be damned if I'll let you take my memories."

"You'll have them back, if that's what you really want, but you should be aware that they're pretty traumatic memories. Think it over. You have an opportunity to start with a clean slate and perhaps—"

"Out of the question."

"Very well. It's up to you. But before we run the program, we should spend some time working out the ghost personality fragments in your matrix. This may be our last chance to debug those glitches, but we'll require more information from you. We can't do it without knowing more about what we're looking for. We'll need your help."

"Forget it."

"You don't understand," she said. "We need to—"

"No, Doctor Stone, *you* don't understand," snapped Steele. "I'll spell it out for you. I want you to put back everything that you took out. *Everything*, you got me? And if I find out you held anything back, I'll go straight to the media and raise a stink like you won't believe! I've *had* it with being your cybernetic guinea pig! You give me back my memories, Doctor, and then stay the hell out of my brain!"

She took a deep breath and let it out slowly. "All right, Steele. Have it your way. But the decision isn't mine to make alone. I simply don't have the authority. I'll have to take it up with Higgins."

"You do that," Steele said. "You tell him to get his ass down here and get the ball rolling. Otherwise you're gonna see another cyborg run amok. You got that?"

"You've made yourself quite clear," she said. "I'm sorry you're taking it this way. Frankly, I think you're making a serious mistake. Instability in your engram matrix could result in schizophrenia. At least let us try to—"

"You're wasting your time, Doctor."

"As you wish." She got up and went to the door. She opened it, then paused briefly. "But this could be your last chance. Don't say I didn't warn you."

Sgt. Tracy was on his way to the guard mount that would relieve the current watch. He wasn't looking forward to it. He had stood guard duty many times in his career, more times than he could count, and it was not one of those things that improved with age. It was a lonely job and, these days, one that could often be dangerous. Especially at night.

At Warren, it consisted of walking a section of the base perimeter that was both fenced and protected by large coils of barbed wire. Like a concentration camp, he thought.

They had opened up several more silos and two more LCFs. More cocked and loaded guns. More corpses. It was grim, nerve-wracking work. And then the maintenance crews went in, ostensibly to verify the status of missiles prior to dismantling them. Ostensibly.

Tracy no longer believed the fiction. Pat Summers no longer believed it. Nor, he was sure, did many of the other soldiers at the base, but no one talked about it. Whatever suspicions they all had, they kept them to themselves. Morale was low. There was a palpable tension in the air. But no one said anything about it. It was as if they didn't want to know.

After eating dinner, Tracy had gone back to his quarters and put on his battle dress for guard duty. Beneath his porous and infrared absorbent outer suit, he wore a lightweight, two-piece undersuit with gloves and socks, all with integral zoned electrical heating controlled by the computer in his backpack. He wore high boots with armored soles and flexible, armored uppers. His full-coverage, dark-visored helmet incorporated a radio, a gyrostabilized laser designator, a thermal imaging camera and an image intensifier, with a visor screen for the projection of data from his video systems as well as computer graphics and aiming marks for his weapons.

He carried a double-barreled polymer/ceramic battle rifle. The upper barrel was capable of firing high explosive shells or shaped charges, smoke-emitting or illuminating shells; the lower barrel fired 4.7mm. caseless ammunition with a select-fire system capability that offered three-round burst, fully automatic or semiautomatic fire. It could be fired manually, using the laser sighting system, but it was also tied in to his helmet and slaved to the targeting system in his backpack computer, which was capable of taking voice-input commands. His weapons system was completed by two rocket launchers, one rocket tube on either side of his backpack, capable of firing short-range missiles launched by voice command. He also carried a holstered polymer/ceramic 9mm. semiauto on his belt, along with magazine and shell pouches and a commando bowie in a self-sharpening sheath. General Cord had given orders that this was to be the uniform for standing guard. He wanted the people under his command to be ready for anything.

What, thought Tracy, did he expect? Surely, no band of outlaw raiders would be crazy enough to attack a military base.

He was halfway to guard mount, carrying his battle rifle in one hand and his helmet under his arm, when a man burst out from between two buildings on his left. He almost ran right into him. The man froze, then glanced quickly over his shoulder. He wasn't in uniform. He wore rumpled civilian clothes. His hair was disheveled, his trousers were torn and he looked terrified.

"Help me, please! For God's sake, you've got to help me! I've got to get out of here! He's crazy! He's—"

"Wait a minute, wait a minute," Tracy said. "Calm down. What are you talking about? Who are you?"

"My name is Franks. Dr. Steven Franks. Please, soldier, you've got to help me! Someone's got to warn them! You don't know what he's planning. He's insane, he's totally insane—"

"Who?"

"*General Cord!* He's planning to take over the government! If they won't do as he says, he intends to launch the missiles! He's going to nuke New York!"

"*What?*"

"All right, hold it right there! *Freeze!*"

"Oh, God, it's too late...."

Tracy looked up to see three Cobras in their dark green, black-trimmed uniforms and black berets moving in on them, their rifles held ready.

"You've got to warn them!" Franks whispered frantically. *Please*, I'm begging you...."

"Put the piece down!"

"Wait a minute!" Tracy shouted. "Take it easy!"

"Put the piece *down!*"

"I'm Sgt. Tracy. I was on my way to—"

"I said put it *down*, right *now!*"

Tracy slowly bent down and put the rifle on the ground, then the helmet.

"Now stand away from him, hands straight out at your sides!"

"Jesus, what *is* it with you guys? Will you for Christ's sake—"

"*Move!*"

Tracy complied.

"All right. Now, Dr. Franks, come along quietly now. Don't make it hard on yourself."

Franks gave him a pleading look, then his shoulders slumped and he turned to walk back toward the men. Two of them fell in beside him and escorted him back to the house where the civilian scientists were quartered. The third approached Tracy, his rifle held waist high, pointed straight at him.

"Hey, come on!" said Tracy. "Lighten up, for God's sake! What's this all about?"

"Tracy, huh?" The Cobra was a lieutenant. The name tag on his breast said MORRIS. He nodded and lowered the gun. "I know you. I've seen you around. What did Franks tell you?"

"Franks? Was that his name? Jeez, I don't know," said Tracy, lying and trying to look confused. "He was babbling something about getting out of here. He was acting crazy. What the hell's going on?"

"That all he said?"

"I don't know what the hell he was yammering about. He kept saying 'I've gotta get out of here,' or something like that. I was on my way to guard mount and he practically ran into me. What was he, drunk?"

"Nervous breakdown," said Morris.

"Jesus," Tracy said, not buying a word of it.

"Yeah. He went out a window on the second floor and just took off. Pressure must've got to him."

"Poor bastard," Tracy said. "Christ, he scared the hell out of me, running out like that. And then you guys came along and . . . shit, for a minute there, I thought you were gonna shoot me!"

"Yeah, well, I'm sorry about that. We had word there were some heavily armed raiders nosing around Cheyenne. Nothing confirmed, but everyone's a little edgy."

Bullshit, Tracy thought, but he tried not to allow his disbelief to show. "Christ, the way he came running out like that, I might've shot him. Jesus. I guess my nerves are a little on edge, too. You wouldn't have a smoke, would you?"

"Sure."

Lt. Morris pulled a pack out of his pocket and handed it to Tracy. He seemed more relaxed now.

"What the hell made him freak out like that?" asked Tracy, anxious to keep the man from thinking that Franks had told him anything.

Morris shrugged. "Who knows? These damn birds've got everybody nervous. Who knows if they'll blow up or not if we crack 'em open? You're one of the guys on entry detail, aren't you?"

"Yeah."

"Then you know what I mean."

"Tell me about it. We opened up two LCFs the other day. Christ, you should've seen the bodies."

"Not a pretty sight, huh?"

"Not hardly. They keep telling us it's safe down there, but like you said, who really knows? Half the guys are going in on sick call every day. They keep thinking that they're coming down with something. Let me tell you, I'll be awful glad when this is over."

"Yeah, well, you can guess how the civilians must be feeling," said Morris. "They're not used to any of this. They came out here from back east, where all this shit is just so much data on paper and now all of a sudden they're lookin' at the real thing. That's why we're keepin' them segregated from the rest of the base personnel. They've got enough to deal with without hearing all the horror stories from the crews opening up the LCFs."

"Yeah, I hear you," said Tracy. "Listen, you think he's gonna be all right? Franks or whatsisname?"

"Yeah, one of the shrinks'll come in and see him. Give him something to calm him down. Little rest, he'll probably be okay. Otherwise, we'll have to ship him home."

"Yeah? You figure if I start running around and screamin', they might ship me home, too?"

Morris chuckled. "I wouldn't count on it."

"Yeah, well, it was an idea. Look, I've got to get going or they'll put me on report."

"Okay. Take it slow. And watch yourself. That rumor about the raiders might be nothing, but you never know."

"Right. I'll keep my eyes open."

"Do that. And listen, about what happened here . . . keep it to yourself, okay? We don't want this getting around. It'd be bad for morale."

"Yeah, I see your point."

"Make sure you do. If I hear any scuttlebutt about this, I'll know where it came from."

"Hey, I didn't see nothin'."

"Good man. Stay loose."

"Right. Thanks for the smoke."

"Don't mention it."

Tracy made it to guard mount with seconds to spare. They marched out to relieve the watch and his stomach was churning all the while. They got to his post and he went out to relieve the guard, then starting slowly walking his post as the guard detail moved away. His brain was full of white noise.

Maybe Morris had been right. Maybe Franks really had freaked out and had a nervous breakdown. But he didn't really believe it. He wanted to, he wanted to desperately, but he couldn't get the sight of the scientist's face out of his mind. That face was etched in fear and desperation. And he knew, with a sinking feeling, that Franks had been telling him the truth. He knew because it all suddenly made sense. Everything simply clicked together. Why there were maintenance crews in all the silos. Why they hadn't dismantled a single missile. Why they hadn't touched anything in any of the LCCs. Why the civilian scientists were kept segregated from the rest of the base personnel, under constant guard, and why the Cobras accompanied every detail into every silo and LCF.

Jesus Christ almighty, he thought. Cord's planning a military coup. And right here at Warren he's got everything he needs to pull it off.

What if they questioned Franks and he broke down and told them what he'd said to him?

Jesus, Tracy thought, I'm scared. I'm really scared.

*"He intends to launch the missiles,"* Franks had said.

That's crazy. That's really fucking crazy....

*"He's insane, he's totally insane...."*

What the hell can I do?

*"Someone's got to warn them!"*

Who do I call? What do I say? They'll think I'm crazy. How can I make them believe me? What if they've got the phones tapped?

*"Yeah, it bothers me,"* Pat Summers had said. *"But what*

*difference does that make? I don't see what we can do about it."*

What if I'm wrong about this?

You're not wrong, said a little voice at the back of his mind. You're not wrong and you know it. It fits. It all fits. It's just the sort of thing that Cord would do. Take charge. Institute martial law, set himself up as a military dictator with his troops and the missiles to back him. Everybody knew he was disgusted with the bureaucrats back east who could never seem to get anything accomplished. Half the time, they couldn't even meet the payroll. . . .

They'll back him, Tracy thought. They'll all back him. Every goddamn military unit in the country. The man's a born leader. Maybe he's even the right man for the job, who was he to say? Who was he to decide? His job was to obey his orders, not to question them. . . .

But what if they didn't listen? What if they called his bluff? He wouldn't really launch the birds, would he?

Yeah. He would. Cord never backed down from anyone or anything. And with so much at stake, he wasn't about to start now.

Tracy's mouth was dry. It was starting to get dark. And he was all alone out here. Alone, right on the base perimeter. . . .

How long would it be before they discovered he was missing?

They'll hunt me down, thought Tracy. They'll send out the SPs and they'll hunt me down. I'd never have a chance. . . .

If he could get to Cheyenne and steal a car, maybe an hour and half or so to Denver, less if he kept it floored . . . he just might make it. They'd look for him in Cheyenne first. If he could get to Denver, he could lose himself. . . .

If they catch you, you'll be shot, you dumb fuck.

I've got no proof, he thought. No proof at all. They'll never believe me. They'll think I'm crazy.

Why *me*? Why does it have to come down to *me*?

If Franks talks, the little voice said, you've had it anyway.

How long? How long have I got? Morris didn't seem to suspect. Maybe Franks won't talk. Maybe he won't say anything. . . .

Go, said the little voice. Go *now*, while you've still got the chance.

Christ. Oh, Christ....

He tossed his rifle up over the fence.

Okay, he thought. Now you've done it. No turning back now....

He started to scale the fence.

Higgins wasn't sure why he felt compelled to do this thing in person. It wasn't as if the man was his friend. In fact, he wasn't sure just what the precise nature of their relationship was. Technically, Ice was an employee, of sorts. An agent, in a sense. Only there were no other agents in the CIA quite like him.

In the old days, Higgins imagined that the "Company," as they had called it back then, had employed a lot of men like Ice. Back when the CIA was like some vast octopus with more tentacles than it could count, the section chiefs had virtually complete autonomy and a free hand to recruit whatever personnel they felt they needed, without ever having to document them on paper. They had informers on their payroll, criminals, assassins, hookers, politicians, businessmen, all "field agents" who reported to their section chiefs directly and who were paid out of the section's budget, which in those days had been allotted without a lot of questions being asked about itemization and expenditures.

It must have been really something back then, thought Higgins. At one time, or so the story went, a new incoming CIA director had requested a complete file on all the personnel working for the agency. He had been told that the request was impossible to grant because nobody really knew. They had absolutely no way of knowing. Back then, the agency had been so large and its structure so incredibly intricate that trying to conduct a census of all its personnel would have been impossible. There were departments within departments, sections within sections within sections.

Section chiefs had field agents they employed that no one knew about except themselves, and in order to guarantee the security of those agents, it was a policy that their identities were never to be revealed to anybody else. Unless special arrangements had been made, new incoming section chiefs did not inherit their predecessor's contacts, but recruited their own people. And those people had their own people, whom they paid off with the section's budget. Boxes within boxes within boxes. The CIA had eyes and ears everywhere.

Now the agency was little more than a tiny bureaucratic arm of a crippled federal government that was fighting for survival. A mere handful of agents and office staff. And soon, it would cease to be even that. Higgins wondered how much time he had left before that bastard Carman brought the axe down. A month? A week? Perhaps only a matter of days or even hours?

And then what?

If he had been an ass kisser, a brown-noser like Harding, there would have been no problem getting reassigned to some nice, cushy post in some other government department, but he wasn't anything like Harding and besides, he didn't want that. He was not a bureaucrat at heart. Jennifer had touched a chord within him and it was vibrating like a tuning fork.

*"The no-man's-land out there is really something. It's big. It's wild. You could be young again...."*

Could he, indeed? Perhaps. The only time in his life that he had truly felt *alive* was when he had been with the Special Operations Group. God, those really had been the days! He had felt a *purpose* then, a vibrancy, a sense of significance and import that he had never truly been able to recapture. Project Download had provided him with a sense that he was doing something, taking part in something important. With Steele, he had once again begun to feel that he was making a contribution that would help to bring the country back together, get it back on the road to becoming the nation it once was.... But still, for all the sense of accomplishment the project gave him, it was not the same. It never could been, not behind a desk.

Jennifer had understood that. She understood him better than any woman he had ever known. Better than *anyone* he had ever known, except, perhaps, one man.

He wondered what Zach Cord was doing now. Last he heard, they had given him command of the entire northwest sector. A few isolated towns and settlements and miles of desolate wilderness, interspersed with bombed out hot spots. And Cord was probably loving every minute of it. He was in his element.

He could have had the job that Higgins had wound up with, but he had turned it down.

"The only thing you can accomplish from behind a desk is to give yourself hemorrhoids and lower back pain," Cord had said contemptuously when he had chosen the option of being transferred to the regular service. "If you're smart, Skeet, you'll stick with me. We'll make our own damn opportunities. We'll find a way to fight it our way, like we always did."

Cord had given him the nickname Skeet, because as a young man, Higgins had been thin as a rake and wiry. One time, Cord and his squad had been pinned down by raiders who had laid down a withering fire with automatic weapons, immobilizing them. Higgins and his squad had pulled him out of it, repeatedly flanking the numerically superior enemy and using hit and run guerrilla tactics, making them think they were up against a much larger force. Later, Cord had compared him to a "pesky skeeter." No matter how many times they slapped at him, Higgins merely darted away and kept on stinging. And the name had stuck.

No one had called him "Skeet" in years. And he hadn't spoken to Zach Cord since the breakup of the SOG, when they had gone their separate ways, Cord to the Army and Higgins to a bureaucratic post at agency headquarters in New York. He had been ambitious then, anxious to move up, but that had been before he found out how stultifying a bureaucrat's life could be. But by the time he learned that, he had already become accustomed to a lifestyle that involved a luxurious apartment, custom-tailored clothes, fine wine and whiskey and meals in the best restaurants in town. He enjoyed the company of beautiful women, and he had a position of respect and responsibility, with a salary that was commensurate with his post. And yet, as the years rolled inexorably by, he came to miss the old days more and more.

Now, it seemed to him that Cord had made the best decision. He was still out there, a general in the forefront of the action, commanding his famous Cobra Force, while Higgins had fallen victim to politics. He was out of a job. And, because he hadn't bothered playing kissy-face with Carman's ample cheeks, there would be no other government post that would enable him to continue to support his lifestyle.

Yet, somehow, that didn't seem so terribly important anymore. He kept thinking about what Jennifer had said about New Mexico.

Could he really start all over once again? A man with his background, with his credentials, would probably have no trouble getting a post with some police force or para-military security outfit. But it had been a long time since he had taken orders. He was much more used to giving them. Perhaps he could set up some sort of independent outfit of his own. He was certainly qualified, and there would be no lack of work. Not out there. The question was, did he really want to go "out there?" With Jennifer?

He had never really had a serious relationship, and incredible though it still seemed, she had never had any sort of relationship at all prior to meeting him. What she said was certainly true. They were both very independent and aggressive personalities who required a lot of space, and they did respect that in each other. But that was here, where they both had separate places to live—though they'd been spending almost all their nights together—and they both had demanding and fulfilling jobs. If she were transferred back to Los Alamos, she'd still have her work, but he'd be starting out from scratch. That could put a lot of pressure on their relationship. And despite the strong attraction that they felt for one another, they really hadn't known each other very long. He still had a lot of doubts. He needed time to think about it. Only he wasn't sure just how much time he had.

Perhaps that was why he felt he had to make this call in person. Because this was another man who'd have the rug yanked out from under him. And though they couldn't be more different, in certain very elemental ways, they were a lot alike. Both fighters. Men who preferred to tackle life on their own terms, but who could take anything life handed out, with no complaints and no regrets. Maybe they weren't exactly friends. Maybe they didn't even like each other very much. But they understood and respected one another. And that was no small thing.

The man who opened the door was huge. He was black, well over six feet tall, with a chest that stretched the tape at 60 inches and arms that measured 24 inches around the biceps.

His flaring lats gave him a dramatic V-shape as they tapered down to a narrow, muscular waist. His head was shaved, and usually he wore dark glasses. However, on this rare occasion, Higgins could see his eyes. And Ice looked even meaner with the shades off.

"Well, well, this be a surprise," he said in a remarkably deep voice that sounded like the crack of doom. "Mr. H. To what I owe the pleasure of this visit?"

"Hello, Ice. Mind if I come in?"

"*Mi casa su casa*," Ice said, stepping aside. "Might as well be. You payin' for it."

"Yes, well, that's what I wanted to talk to you about."

"Have a seat," said Ice. "Drink?"

"No thanks. I won't be long."

He sat down on the couch. Ice settled his giant frame in a chair across from him. As usual, he was dressed all in black, with a minimal amount of jewelry. Just a heavy gold ring and a gold chain around his neck, a small gold skull dangling from it, a keepsake from his days as leader of the Skulls. The apartment was fairly Spartan. Just a couch, two large and comfortable lounge chairs, a lamp, a coffee table and a television set. The dining room had a table and four chairs. The kitchen had a smaller table, some chairs and a refrigerator. The bedroom had a large, queen-sized bed, two nightstands and a bureau. All were furnishings that had come with the place. Ice had done absolutely nothing to make it his own.

The walls were bare. The place had a sort of bleakness about it. And yet, unless he was on a job for the agency, which usually meant working with Steele, he did not go out much. Apparently he did a lot of reading, although he didn't keep the books. He either borrowed them or bought them and then sold them as soon as he had read them. His tastes, surprisingly, ran to the classics, which didn't really jibe with his style of street talk and his hardcase image. Clearly, there was a lot more to him than met the eye, though Higgins had never been able to penetrate the cold and implacable exterior that Ice presented to the world. It was like trying to get to know a statue.

The first time they had met, there had been a contract out on Ice. For years, he had been a wanted criminal, the leader of the most powerful street gang in the no-man's-land just north of Midtown, the area known as Harlem. Nothing at all was known about his background, and Ice didn't volunteer any information. No one even knew his real name. Under his leadership, the Skulls had become a powerful force in no-man's-land, either subjugating or driving out most of the competing gangs, but when crime boss Victor Borodini made his bid to bring the street gangs under his control, Ice had resisted. Borodini closed a deal with a younger faction of the Skulls, and Ice wound up squeezed out and on the run, with a large contract on his life. And it was then that Ice approached the federal authorities with an offer to help them nail Borodini and neutralize his operations.

A meeting was set up in an abandoned storefront out in no-man's-land and the man sent out to negotiate with the former leader of the Skulls had been Donovan Steele. But Ice had been betrayed, and Borodini's soldiers hit the storefront moments after Steele had arrived. Ice managed to escape, but Steele was shot down and left for dead. It was that event which led to his being reconstructed as a cyborg. Shortly thereafter, Ice came in out of the cold and met with Higgins. In exchange for his cooperation with the authorities, he was given amnesty and placed on the agency's payroll. Together, Ice and Steele had dismantled Victor Borodini's operations in the city and taken down his heavily protected enclave out in Cold Spring Harbor. At first, Higgins had had his doubts about him, but the big man had played straight with him right from the beginning, and now Higgins figured that the least he could do was return the favor.

"I'm afraid I've got bad news," he said, "and I wanted to let you know in person. After what happened with Stalker, the committee decided to cut our funding. We're being shut down. They're taking Download away from the agency, and the cyborg project is being scrapped. They don't want any repetition of what happened with Stalker. At least, that's the excuse they're using. What it all comes down to is that without Download, and with the cyborg project shut down, the agency's no longer doing anything that can't be handled by the military or by other government departments. So it looks like we're going to be disbanded."

"I see," said Ice. "So I be outta work, huh?"

"Yeah." Higgins nodded. "Most of the other agency personnel will probably be transferred to other departments, but your case is somewhat... uh, special. Given your background, I don't see them being too anxious to find another slot for you. I don't really know what I can do, but I can try to pull some strings get you a job with a security branch somewhere, or maybe give you a recommendation to Strike Force. I'm not completely without influence and—"

Ice gave a short, barking laugh. "Me? A po-lice man? I don't think Chief Hardesty be too happy 'bout that. And I look damn silly in a uniform. No, I think I pass."

"Well, I'm not sure what else I can do for you," Higgins said. "And I'd like to be able to do *something*. I owe you at least that much."

"You don't owe me nuthin', Mr. H. We had us a deal. I help you, you give me a crack at Victor Borodini. You done that. We square."

"You'll have to give up this apartment," Higgins said. "They'll be asking you to leave soon. Where will you go?"

"I come up with somethin'. Always have."

"I'm sorry about this, Ice. They're cutting me loose, too. I've made too many enemies. But while I'm still in office, is there anything that I can do for you? Anything at all?"

Ice shook his head. "Don't worry about me, Mr. H. I take care of myself. This straight life not really my scene, anyway. But I appreciate the offer. What you gonna do?"

"I don't know yet," Higgins said. "I may be heading out west, to New Mexico. See if I can remember what it's like to get my hands dirty." He paused. "Look, why don't you consider coming with me? I'm probably going to put together some kind of private outfit of my own out there. I could use a good man like you."

"Well, that's mighty white of you," said Ice with a big smile. "But I be a city boy. I done grew up here. I think I stick around. Maybe I put together somethin' of my own, too."

"What, another gang?"

"Why not? Maybe I look in on the Skulls again. Hear they not doin' so well since I left."

Higgins shook his head. "That would be a waste, Ice. What kind of life is that? You can do better for yourself. Look, it's your life. I'm not going to try to tell you what to do. You've always played straight with me and I appreciate that. You helped us take Borodini down and I'd like to return the favor. At least think about what I said, okay? I'll keep the offer open."

Ice nodded. "I do that. What about Steele?"

"I don't know. I suppose he'll probably wind up back with Strike Force. And if you go back to no-man's-land, it'll put you two on opposite sides. I'd really hate to see that happen."

Ice pursed his lips thoughtfully and nodded. "Yeah. That be too bad."

"Well, look, I've said my piece. Give it some thought. You've done some real good, Ice. I'd hate to see you throw it all away by getting back on the wrong side of the law."

"Law didn't do all that much for you, did it?"

"It wasn't the law that did me in," said Higgins, thinking of Carman. "It was the lawyers. There's a big difference."

"Steele gonna be comin' back?"

"Yes, we'll be releasing him before too long. I've got to go back and see him. I expect he'll have a thing or two to say to me."

"Ask him to stop by," said Ice.

"I'll do that."

He got up and Ice walked him to the door. Higgins paused. "Look, just in case we don't see each other again . . . well, I'd like to wish you luck."

"You too, Mr. H." He smiled. "For a fed, you not so bad."

Higgins smiled and offered him his hand. They shook. "Take care of yourself."

As he walked down the hall toward the elevator, he wondered if he'd ever see the big man again. It was strange. They came from completely different backgrounds and had almost nothing in common. And in the old days, back when he'd still been with Cord in SOG, they'd have been deadly enemies. Yet in a funny sort of way, he was going to miss him.

# 4

General Zachary Cord cut an imposing figure. He stood five-feet-eleven in his stocking feet and he had a trim, muscular build. He was fifty-two years old, but he looked much younger. His dark hair was only beginning to streak with gray, and his cornflower blue eyes were sharp and alert. He looked like a hero, handsome, with a strong jaw and chisled facial features. He was like a coiled spring, all controlled tension, and he spoke in a clipped, authoritative manner.

"How much did Franks tell him?"

"Enough," said his executive officer, Col. Seth Tyler of the Cobra Force. Tyler was about five-eight, well-built, with sandy blond hair and hazel eyes. Like his commander, he was in peak condition, and he held himself with the tight bearing of a professional soldier. "As soon as the security commander found out that Franks had talked to one of the regular personnel, he sent some men out to bring Sgt. Tracy in for questioning. That's when they found out he wasn't at his post. They reported back to Lt. Royce and he sent a detail out to look for him, just in case Tracy decided to slip off to the latrine or something.

Then he questioned Franks again. Franks tried to deny he said anything at first, but he broke down pretty easily. Apparently, he spilled enough to Tracy that he believed it and went over the wall."

"Why wasn't I notified immediately?" snapped Cord.

"Royce didn't want to start ringing the bell until he was sure there was a fire. The obvious place for Tracy to go was into Cheyenne, so he sent a squad of SPs to look for him. He figured Tracy would be easy to run down. He was on foot and dressed in full combat gear. That would make him pretty conspicuous. They followed the most direct route Tracy would have taken, and they found a little bar where Tracy stole a car out of the lot. He hot-wired it and took off. Some locals gave pursuit, but Tracy fired off a few bursts and discouraged them. My guess is he'll probably make for Denver. We've sent a chopper out to intercept him. We don't know if he managed to get to a phone, but even if he did call anybody, his story would've sounded pretty wild. And he's got no proof."

"It doesn't matter," Cord said. "We have to assume we're blown. How close are we to being operational?"

"Keeping a good safety margin, maybe a couple of days, at most."

"All right. We'll proceed on schedule. I want a full assembly at reveille tomorrow. I'm going to address the troops. All liberties are cancelled as of now. I want every man in Cobra Force to turn out under arms and I want the armory secured."

"What about Tracy?"

"I want him brought back here. That man deserted while we were under full alert, and I intend to make an example of him. Nobody goes AWOL under my command. Nobody."

"You gonna court-martial him?"

"No, Colonel, the man's a damn deserter and a traitor. I'm going to hang him."

The old black Ford pickup had seen better days, but though the body was badly rusted, scratched and dented, the dash console cracked and the seats torn, its owner had taken pains to keep its powerful V-8 engine in good running order by scavenging parts from other old, dilapidated cars. The hood had been removed, exposing a cobbled-together motor that looked as if it were held together with bailing wire and spit. Jury-rigged wiring; crude, homemade carburetor manifold; patched-up radiator; the whole thing looked like some kind of weird, Rube Goldberg contraption with parts and hoses sticking out all over the damn place, but, amazingly enough, it ran and it ran well. It made a sound something like a cross between an old World War I biplane engine and a high-speed motorboat, a raspy, throaty *thraaaaaaagggh* as Tracy pushed it to its limits, keeping the accelerator pedal floored and punishing the shocks as the truck hurtled down the cracked and buckled roadbed of I-25, heading south toward Denver.

He had stolen it from outside a small bar in Cheyenne, but with the roar that the damn thing made, the theft had been discovered within seconds of his having hot-wired the ignition. The owner and several of his friends had come piling out of the bar as he was backing the behemoth dualie out of its parking space, where it was surrounded by similarly dilapidated heaps, and as he spun the wheel, they had opened up on him with their revolvers and semiautomatics.

He had ducked down behind the wheel and gunned it as the passenger side window, already starred with cracks, shattered as the bullets struck it. Then, as he got the big truck turned around, the rear window exploded into the cab from the hail of .44 magnum, .357 and 9mm. rounds, most of which continued through and smashed the windshield. As the truck slewed out of the gravelled lot, its owner and his friends had piled into several other cars to give pursuit. Driving one-handed, Tracy had stuck the barrel of his battle rifle out the rear window of the cab and fired several bursts on full auto, purposely aiming high so as not to hit any of them. That had discouraged his pursuers, but by now, he was certain that the base knew of his desertion, and it would be a simple matter for them to connect it with the theft of the truck. So he was expecting pursuit.

And as he passed the turnoff for Loveland, they caught up to him.

He drove with his battle helmet on as protection from the wind blast that came in through the shot-out windshield as he pushed the truck to about a hundred miles an hour. With the wind and the roar of the truck's monster engine, he didn't hear the chopper coming up behind him until the .50 caliber machine gun rounds stitched the roadbed on either side of him. The X-wing chopper passed overhead, swooping low with its lights on. The pickup veered and he almost lost control, sliding onto the shoulder, the rear end slipping around as he fought the wheel to get the truck back on the road.

The chopper gained altitude and turned, coming straight back at him as it made another strafing run. Once more, the machine guns opened up, bracketing him as the chopper made its second pass. Tracy gritted his teeth and swore. They were trying to get him to pull over. If they wanted to, they could have blasted him into oblivion on their first pass. And if he didn't stop, they would. There was no way he could outrun them. And there wasn't anywhere to hide.

He hit the brakes and the truck skidded, the tires braking loose as it came around sideways, Tracy fighting the wheel and turning in the direction of the skid to keep from flipping over. He didn't stop to shut the engine off, he hurled himself out the door, grabbing his backpack and battle rifle. He could see the X-wing chopper turning for a third run.

With the truck momentarily blocking him from their view, he quickly strapped on the backpack, plugged in his helmet and activated his weapons systems computer. He had only one chance. He spoke into his helmet mike.

"Rocket launcher, target approximately one hundred meters and closing, ready one rocket. . . ."

The aiming marks appeared on the screen inside his visor, and he lined them up visually with a quick movement of his head.

"Lock on target. . . ."

The computer immediately began to display the aiming data, distance, elevation and trajectory, speed of target. . . .

"Stand by. . . ."

The chopper was starting to swoop down.

*"Fire!"*

He braced himself as the rocket ignited and left its tube, arcing up directly at the chopper. The range was too close. The chopper pilot never had a chance. The helicopter exploded in a fireball as the rocket struck, raining flaming debris down on the deserted highway. Tracy's stomach contracted. He tore his helmet off and threw up on the road.

He continued to have dry heaves long after he had spewed his guts out. He leaned weakly against the truck and tried to tell himself that he'd had no other choice, it was them or him, but that still didn't make it any easier. He had killed his fellow soldiers. Now, in addition to desertion, he was guilty of murder. He threw the backpack into the cab and climbed in, breathing heavily, gulping in air. He was shaking.

"Come on," he said to himself out loud. "Come *on*, pull yourself together, damn it!"

He slammed the truck in gear and peeled out toward Denver.

The phone on Linda Tellerman's desk rang and she picked it up. It was the operator downstairs.

"Miss Tellerman, I've got a collect person-to-person call for you from a Sergeant Reese Tracy of the 3rd Division, Northwest Command. He says it's extremely important. Will you accept it?"

Linda frowned. She didn't know anybody by that name. Northwest Command. That would be General Cord, she thought. They had done a story on him recently. He had been placed in charge of dismantling the ICBM network out in that part of the country.

"I'll take the call."

"One moment, I'll switch you.... Go ahead, sir."

"Miss Tellerman?"

"This is Linda Tellerman. What can I do for you, Sergeant ... Tracy, is it?"

"Listen, you don't know me, but I saw the stories you did on that CIA cyborg that went out of control. You had the guts to take on the government. You weren't intimidated."

"Thank you, Sergeant, I appreciate that, but—"

"Please don't interrupt, just listen. I was stationed out at Warren Air Force Base. General Cord is *not* dismantling the missiles out there. There are maintenance crews in every silo and LCF we've opened up so far, with commandos of the Cobra Force to watch over them. They're—"

"Wait a moment," she said. "Back up a little. What do you mean he's not dismantling the missiles? Is there some sort of problem?"

"*Listen*, for God's sake! The LCFs all received their launch codes, back when the launch order was given during the war. Those missiles that weren't launched are still standing ready in their silos, because the launch crews succumbed to the plague before they could fully carry out their launch procedures. We were supposed to open up the silos and the LCFs, stand the missiles down and then dismantle them. But Cord isn't doing that. He intends to launch them!"

She frowned. "What the hell is this, some kind of joke?"

"Miss Tellerman, this is no joke, I swear to God! General Cord has got all the civilian scientists they sent out to supervise the project. He's keeping them prisoner, under armed guard. One of them got away tonight, and I had a chance to speak with him before he was recaptured. His name was Franks. Doctor Steven Franks."

She still thought it was some kind of crank call, but purely by force of habit, Linda wrote down "Dr. Steven Franks" on the pad in front of her.

"He was trying to get off the base, Miss Tellerman," Tracy continued. "He escaped out a second-story window and managed to get past the guards. He just happened to run into me as I was on my way to guard duty. He was scared to death, Miss Tellerman. He was trying to get out to warn somebody. He said Cord's gone insane. He's planning a military coup. He's brought in special units from all around the country, Rangers and Delta Force, and merged them with the Cobra Force. The base is on full alert. Cord intends to use the missiles to blackmail the government into giving him control. If they won't do as he demands, he'll drop a Peacemaker on New York! And there are enough missiles still standing in their silos for him to take out Boston, Chicago, Detroit, Atlanta, all the government centers. Once they've been retargeted and he's got them operational, there won't be any way to stop him. Even if the regular military personnel out here refuse to back him up, it won't do any good. The Cobra Force is in complete control of the base. No one gets issued any arms unless they're on guard duty or out working on the silos. And, frankly, the way things have been going, I'm not sure the regular troops wouldn't go along with him. Most of them haven't been paid for weeks. There won't be anything to prevent him from seizing control of the government and establishing a military dictatorship."

"That's an astonishing allegation, Sergeant. Can you actually *prove* any of this?"

"I knew you'd ask me that," said Tracy with exasperation. "No, I can't prove a word of it. All I've got is what Franks told me. And what I've seen for myself. Look, I was on one of the details assigned to open up the missile silos and the LCFs. And we haven't dismantled any of them! Not a single one! There are crews in there making repairs, replacing equipment and running checks on all the systems. The underground cables connecting the LCFs to the silos are still in good shape. None of the warheads have been removed. None of the consoles have been deactivated. I can't prove any of this to you over the phone, Miss Tellerman, but you've *got* to believe me! You've got to tell the right authorities. Maybe they can check it out somehow. They've got to be warned. Look, I know how wild this must sound. You probably think I'm crazy or this is all some kind of hoax, but ask yourself, can you really afford to take that chance?"

"Where are you calling from, Sergeant Tracy?"

"I'm calling from Denver. I was on guard duty tonight and I went AWOL. I don't know how much time I've got, but they'll be coming after me. They've already tried to get me once. They sent a chopper out to intercept me on the road, and I had to shoot it down. By now, they've probably gotten word to the police here. If they catch me, I'm dead."

"All right, calm down, Tracy. Assuming you *are* telling me the truth, how can I get in touch in with you again?"

"You can't. I'm not sure where I'll be. And no offense, Miss Tellerman, but I don't think it would be smart for me to tell anybody where I could be found. Look, it's not that I don't trust you, but I'm scared. I'm scared to death. I'm all alone out here. But I'll call you back in about two hours. That should give you enough time to see if you can check this out somehow. Please, Miss Tellerman, you've got to take this seriously. A lot of the people up at Warren have felt strange about what was going on. We thought maybe Cord had special orders to bring the missiles back on line, but none of us ever figured on anything like this! Most of the people up there don't even know what Cord is up to. I couldn't think who else to call. I figured the news media would be my best chance to get the word out, and you were the only person I could think of. You've *got* to do something! *Please!*"

"All right, Tracy, calm down. I'll look into it and see what I can do. Maybe I can help you. I've got connections in Denver through the network. But if you're jerking my chain on this, all bets are off, you understand?"

"I understand."

"You'll be back in touch?"

"In about a couple of hours, if I'm lucky. If you don't hear from me by then, it means I'm probably dead."

"Okay, Tracy. Get back to me as soon as you can. Good luck."

"Thanks. I'll need it."

She heard the click and then hung up the phone. She took a deep breath and let it out slowly. Jesus Christ, she thought. If this is on the level. . . .

She picked up the phone again and dialed an extension in the building, calling down to the research department.

"Randy? It's Linda. I need you to check something out for me and I need it yesterday. Find out everything you can about a Doctor Steven Franks. That name seems to ring a bell. See if we've done any stories on him. He could be a government scientist of some sort, currently at Warren Air Force Base out in Wyoming. I need to verify that, if possible, and I need it ASAP?"

"Okay, I'll get right on it."

She hung up the phone and lit a cigarette. Then she picked it up again and called Randy back.

"Randy? Linda again. Have somebody check and see if there's been any recent concentration of military units at Warren. Especially elite troops, like Ranger or Delta Force units."

"What are you onto?"

"I don't know yet. But I just got a tip, and if it checks out, we're going to have one hell of a story on our hands, so get cracking, okay?"

"You got it."

She hung up the phone and sat for a moment, drumming her fingers on her desk. She bit her lower lip, and then decided.

She picked up the phone and dialed a number at the Federal Building.

"Central Intelligence Agency."

"This is Linda Tellerman, Eyewitness News," she said. "Let me speak to Oliver Higgins."

"One moment, please."

She waited.

"I'm sorry, Miss Tellerman, Mr. Higgins isn't available right now. Can I take a message?"

"Tell him that it's *absolutely vital* that he get back to me as soon as possible," she said. "He's got my number. Tell him I've got some very important information for him. It could be a matter of national security."

"Would you like me to connect you with Director Harding's office?"

She thought quickly. No, Harding wasn't the right man for something like this. Even if he took it seriously, he'd only pass it on to someone else, and by the time anything was done about it, then if what Tracy said was true, it could be too late.

"No, I have to speak to Higgins personally. Please tell him it's really important."

"I'll be sure he gets your message as soon as he comes in, Miss Tellerman."

"Please tell him to call me as soon as possible. Thank you."

She hung up the phone. Maybe it was all some sort of hoax, she thought, but Tracy did sound scared. And just in case it wasn't, this was no time to sit on information like this. If it was true, they'd have to evacuate the city. Only *how*? And even if they could evacuate New York, there was nothing to prevent Cord from striking at Boston or Chicago or Detroit or. . . .

Her phone rang and she snatched it up.

"Linda Tellerman."

"Linda, it's Randy. I've got some of that information for you; I'm still working on the rest. Want me to boot it up to you?"

"Go ahead," she said, turning on her computer. Seconds later, the file on Dr. Steven Vincent Franks appeared on the screen. Graduate of M.I.T. with a degree in nuclear physics. Specialist in strategic weapons. Attached to the Department of

Defense.... She held her breath as she scanned the data on the screen. There was a notation at the bottom of the file that they had recently done a story on him. She took down the file number, called the video library and had them rush the cassette to her desk. As soon as it was delivered, she inserted it into her VCR. The reporter who had done the interview was Steve Howard. She fast-forwarded past his intro and stopped when Franks started speaking.

"... past time that we brought our attention to this," Franks was saying, "but now that General Cord has got the area well under control, we'll be able to go in and start the dismantling procedure."

"Will it be dangerous, Doctor?"

"Well, there will be certain hazards, of course, but there's really no cause for alarm. Once we've gained access to the launch control facilities, it'll be a matter of ascertaining the status of the missiles and the electrical equipment, but I can assure the public that with trained specialists present on the scene, and General Cord's troops providing the security, there is absolutely no chance whatsoever of an accidental launch. There were numerous redundancies built into the Peacekeeper system designed to prevent just that. If the equipment is still in order, which is somewhat doubtful, we'll simply use it to stand the missiles down and then we can proceed with dismantling them. If not, then with the power down, it will be a relatively simple matter to pull the panels and deactivate the consoles. The primary hazards that we'll be encountering will be with residual radiation, when we have to go into the silos and the LCFs that are located in hot spots, but with protective clothing and the proper precautions, those hazards should be fairly minor. In any case—"

Linda stopped the tape. Her mouth had gone dry and she had a sinking feeling in her stomach. So far, it was all checking out. True, Tracy or whoever he was could have seen that report and gotten Franks' name from there, but still.... Her phone rang again.

"Linda? Randy again. I've got some of that other stuff for you. You were right. There were a number of special combat units recently transferred to General Cord's command out at Warren, at his request, to provide additional security for the dismantling of the missiles out there. The 1st Ranger Battalion out of Seattle, a Delta Force unit out of Langley—"

"Jesus Christ," said Linda, under her breath.

"What is it? What've you got?"

"I can't talk now, Randy. I've got to get off the phone. Thanks loads."

"Don't mention it. Listen, let me know what you come up with."

"Believe me, you'll know," she said.

"Okay, start the run," said Higgins.

Jennifer punched the code into the console. "Okay. Engram data's being loaded."

They stared through the window of the isolation room at Steele, lying on his back on the laboratory couch. His eyes were open. As the run was initiated, he started to blink rapidly as the engram data was transmitted directly to his cybernetic brain.

"Well, I hope it's what he really wanted," Higgins said. "We probably won't have a chance to modify his programming again. I just got the word a few minutes ago. They're shutting us down as of tomorrow."

Jennifer glanced up at him, eyes wide. "So *soon*?"

Higgins grimaced. "Carman's not taking any chances," he said. "He's moving fast to make sure the committee doesn't have a chance to change its mind."

Jennifer sighed. "All that work. And it was all for nothing."

"Maybe not," said Higgins. "They're keeping Download operational. They'll be moving the project headquarters to Los Alamos, to combine it with the lab there, which was about what we figured they'd do. And you're the logical person to head it up. So you'll be going home, and all this equipment will probably be going with you. Along with all the data it contains. And any hitchhikers."

She gave him a sharp look. "You mean the backup matrix?"

He nodded. "They still don't know about the matrix and that could be our ace in the hole. Maybe it's still not too late to play it."

"Assuming it's still here," she said. "I've had two teams

running search programs around the clock and they haven't found it yet."

"You haven't found it, but it's here," said Higgins. "It's right here in this lab somewhere, hiding out in one of the data banks. Hiding and waiting."

She looked uneasy. "Waiting for what?"

"For answers, maybe. There's still a lot it doesn't know, and this is where all the answers are. Here, and in that room right there." He looked through the window at Steele. "Besides," he added, "where else would it go?"

"After what I've seen it do, I'm not so sure it couldn't go anywhere it wanted to," she replied. "Through the power lines or the phone lines... maybe it's already gone. The greatest scientific discovery of the century and we've lost it."

"We haven't lost it yet," Higgins said. "I've been talking to Dev Cooper. And I'm finally beginning to understand it all. He's spent a lot of time with the matrix and he knows it. And the key is that there's virtually no difference between Steele and the matrix, except that Steele's got a body and the matrix doesn't. And Steele's experienced some things that the matrix hasn't. Or at least, it's never had a chance to... until right now."

For a second, she stared at him, puzzled, and then comprehension dawned.

"The program run!" she said.

"That's right. Everything that Steele knows that the matrix doesn't is all contained right there," said Higgins, indicating the data bank that was loading Steele's own memories back into his cybernetic brain. "And whatever's not in there...." he turned and looked through the window into the room where Steele lay, "... is right in there. It's an opportunity I don't think the matrix can pass up."

"My God, you did all this on purpose! You set this up!"

"We were running out of time," said Higgins. "Carman didn't give me any other choice. That matrix is the heart and soul of this entire project. It's everything we've worked for, but it's incomplete. And what's more, the matrix knows it. It knows that it's only a copy of Steele's original engrams, and it knows that while it was in storage, Steele's been out there, living a life and having experiences that it knows nothing about. I'm banking on my knowledge of Steele's nature. We took some very painful memories from him, but you saw how he reacted. Just the way I knew he would. He wanted them back. He won't give up any part of himself, even if it means living with pain and cybernetic ghosts. And I'm betting that the matrix is no different. It wants an identity. It wants a life. It wants to be complete. Well, here's its chance. Let's see what it does."

"But what about Steele?" Jennifer swallowed nervously. "What if it decides to insinuate itself into the run? It's overridden our commands before. What if it tries to . . . to take him over? We might not be able to stop it!"

"So what?" said Higgins with a shrug. "What difference would it make? It's a backup copy of Steele's own mental engrams. It wouldn't change him any. He'd still be the same person."

"We don't know that," she said. "No, it's much too risky. I'm cutting out of the run right now."

"Don't!" Higgins grabbed her hands as she reached for the console. "Let's see if it will take the bait! We may not have another chance!"

"And if Steele's programming is damaged, we won't have another chance to fix it," she said. "I'm not going to risk it." She twisted away from him and terminated the broadcast link. "He's absolutely right. We've got no right to. . . ." She frowned suddenly. "What the hell?"

"What is it?"

"The program is still running!" She punched the keys, reentering the code. "I'm getting no response!"

"It's the matrix!" Higgins said. "I knew it! It's taken the bait!"

Jennifer kept punching the keys. "Nothing's happening! I've lost control!"

"Trace it!" Higgins said excitedly. "See where it's coming from!"

*"How?"*

"It's right here in the lab somewhere. It's got to be receiving the data somewhere! Shut down! Shut down all the data banks! The one that won't respond, that's where the matrix is!"

Jennifer got up from the console and shouted out to all the

personnel in the huge lab. "Attention! Everyone, whatever you're doing, shut down! Shut down right *now*! Shut down *immediately*!"

She looked back at the screen on her console, watching the data blurring past as the program run progressed at high speed. One by one, the other computers in the lab started to shut down.

"I want everything in this entire lab shut down!" Higgins shouted. "I want to know if anything is still running!"

A moment later, one of the engineers turned from his console. "Sir, I've got a malfunction here. I'm getting no response."

"*Bingo!*"

They both ran across the lab.

"I can't understand it," said the puzzled engineer, entering commands with his keyboard without any result. "It's not responding to input commands. I can't shut it off. I was able to get out of the program I was running, but suddenly this came up, and I don't know what the hell it is."

Data was flickering past on his screen, faster than the eye could follow.

"*Gotcha!*" Higgins said. He glanced up at the racks behind the console. "Okay, now, quick, while it's still running, pull the back off and—"

Suddenly one of the data banks on the other side of the lab came on line, all of its own accord.

"Dr. Stone!" shouted a technician. "This one just came on line all by itself!"

And then another one came on. And then another and another, as the matrix seemed to leap from one computer to another, traveling with incredible speed through the power lines buried in the floor.

"*Damn it!*" Higgins swore, watching helplessly as all the data banks in the lab started to go on and off, as if animated by gremlins. And then, suddenly, the screen before them flickered on once more, only instead of data flashing past in a blur, it displayed an image of Oliver Higgins and Jennifer Stone, on the desk up in his office, her skirt hiked high above her waist. . . .

*"Jesus!"* Higgins snatched up a phone and hurled it through the screen.

The CRT exploded in a shower of sparks.

The engineer beside them was staring in astonishment. Higgins glared at him and stared him down.

"Excuse me," the man said, clearing his throat uneasily. "I . . . I just remembered . . . there was something I had to do. . . ."

Furious, Higgins turned on his heel and stalked out of the lab.

"Christ. *Steele!*" said Jennifer. She had forgotten all about him.

She hurried back to the isolation room where she had left Steele and flung open the door. He was sitting up, rubbing his temples with his fingertips. He looked up as she burst in.

"Steele! Are you all right?"

He sighed. "No, not really. But I suppose I will be, in time." He smiled sadly. "I remember it all now. Thank you, Doctor."

He got up and walked past her, out the door.

Higgins stormed into his office, past his secretary, who tried to speak to him, but he didn't even pause as he went past her and slammed the door. He went straight over to the bar and poured himself a stiff drink.

"Damn it," he said. *"Damn it!"*

He felt furious, frustrated and completely helpless. The matrix had him at its mercy. Short of tearing up the floors and ripping out all the power lines in the lab, there was no way to stop it. Even if they tried that, it could use the phone lines to get out of the lab before they could shut off all avenues of escape. He could order all the power in the building shut down and risk the wrath of the entire federal bureaucracy, but the matrix could gain access to the security control center and override him. It could always stay several steps ahead, as it had just graphically demonstrated to him, and that little porno display it had put on, with him and Jennifer as the stars, was as clear a warning as he'd ever seen.

*Back off. Or else.*

It was like fighting Steele. It *was* fighting Steele, pitting himself against Steele's electronic twin, and Steele was smart and Steele was fast and Steele could be ruthless and the matrix could do things that Steele never even dreamed of. Higgins glanced up at the security surveillance camera mounted up near the ceiling in the corner of his office. The camera was pointing straight at him. The little red light was on.

"*Damn you!*" he shouted, hurling his glass at the lens. He missed and it shattered against the wall.

His intercom buzzed.

"Mr. Higgins?"

His secretary.

Now what?

He switched it on. "Yes, Nancy, what is it?" he snapped.

"I'm sorry to disturb you, sir, but there's a call for you from Linda Tellerman of Eyewitness News. She's left several messages, and I've got her on the phone right now. She says its extremely urgent, a matter of national security. Do you wish to speak with her?"

"*National security?*" said Higgins. "What the hell's she trying to pull now? Christ, put her on."

He switched on the speaker phone, ready to vent all his anger and frustration on the newswoman.

"What is it *now*, Miss Tellerman?" he snapped. "Jesus, you media people don't care what the hell you say as long as it gets you what you want, do you? If you're going to throw terms like 'national security' around, you'd damn well better—"

"Higgins, shut up and *listen* to me!"

The abruptness and the fierce intensity of her reply took him aback momentarily and he fell silent.

"I've got reason to believe that New York's in danger of being struck by an ICBM," she said.

"*What?* Are you crazy? What the *hell* are you talking about?"

"Just listen to me and don't interrupt. About an hour and a half ago, I had a call from a Sgt. Reese Tracy, of the 3rd Division, Northwest Command, stationed out at Warren Air Force Base in Wyoming. That's General Zachary Cord's command. They're supposed to be dismantling the missiles out there, but Tracy said they've opened up a number of silos and Launch Control Facilities and they haven't dismantled a single one. He said the base is on full alert. There are maintenance crews in all the silos and the LCFs they've opened up, running checks on all the systems and putting in new computer modules. He told me the scientists who were sent out to supervise the project are all being kept prisoner by General Cord's Cobra Force, but one of them got out and spoke to him. He said that Cord was planning a military coup and that he was going to use the missiles to blackmail the government into giving him control. And if they didn't give in to his demands, he was going to drop a Peacekeeper on Midtown."

For a moment, Higgins was stunned into silence. Then he burst out laughing.

"What the hell have you been smoking?" he said. "That's the most ridiculous thing I've ever heard. I happen to know Zach Cord, Miss Tellerman. I served with him in the Special Operations Group. The man's a patriot of the first rank. Somebody's been pulling your leg. I thought you were too good a reporter to fall for a cock 'n' bull story like that, for cryin' out loud!"

"I know it sounds crazy, Higgins. I didn't believe it, either. But I looked into it. Tracy said the name of the scientist he spoke to was Doctor Steven Franks. I ran a check on him. We recently did an interview with him, and he was one of the people the government sent out to Warren to supervise the dismantling of the missiles."

"If you did an interview with this Franks guy, your caller probably saw it and got the name from there," said Higgins.

"Yes, I thought of that, too, but he also said that Cord had brought in special units from other military bases around the country. Rangers and Delta Force. We never reported anything like that. I looked into it and it was true. A battalion of Rangers was sent out to Warren from Seattle, at Cord's own request. And a Delta Force unit went out to Warren from Langley. Why does Cord need elite military units like that just to provide extra security when he's already got the Cobra Force and the regular troops under his command? I ran a check on Tracy, too. There *is* a Staff Sergeant Reese Tracy attached to the 3rd Division of the Northwest Command at Warren. He's part of a unit that recently came up from Denver, and he's been reported AWOL. The Denver police have been alerted to look out for him. Everything he told me checks out. I also tried calling General Cord out at Warren, but they wouldn't put my call through."

"Yeah, well, I can hardly blame them."

"Higgins, I've been in this business for a long time, and I've picked up a damn good instinct for telling whether or not a tip is on the level. This one is legit. I can feel it in my gut."

"Your gut, huh?" Higgins snorted. "All right, Miss Tellerman, I'll check it out. What the hell, I haven't spoken to Zach Cord in a long time. We can probably have a good laugh over this."

"Well, before you start laughing, Franks told Tracy that General Cord has gone insane. Tracy went AWOL to get the word out. He said he'd try to call me again in about two hours, unless they ran him down and killed him first. If he's still okay, I should be hearing from him any time. All right, maybe this is a cock 'n' bull story, as you put it. Tracy himself said it sounded crazy and he had no proof. But he also asked me if I could afford to take the chance that it wasn't on the level. Can you?"

She sounded frightened. Higgins frowned. He knew Linda Tellerman. She was a tough street reporter and she didn't frighten easily. She also wasn't gullible.

"And here's something else for you to think about," she said. "Tracy said they sent a chopper out to intercept him on the road to Denver. He said he had to shoot it down. I've confirmed that. The Denver Strike Force was informed that he was unbalanced, armed with a full battle kit and dangerous. They were told to take no chances, that he had already shot down an X-wing chopper with a rocket launcher. Why would they bother to send out an attack helicopter after only one deserter? Doesn't that seem a little like overkill to you?"

"All right, Miss Tellerman. I'll look into it. Frankly, I think this is the craziest thing I've ever heard, but I'll check it out, okay? And if this Tracy character calls you back, you find out where he is and tell him to stay put, then call me right away."

"Forget it. I'm not going to jeopardize my source. For all I know, you'll turn him right over to your buddy, Cord."

"All right, if you don't trust me, then give him my number and tell him to call me."

She hesitated. "Okay, I can do that. But I'll warn him about a trace."

"Fine," said Higgins with a grimace. "You do that."

"I'm still investigating this, Higgins. I didn't *have* to call you, you know. But like Tracy said, I didn't want to take the chance that he wasn't on the level. As far as I'm concerned, I've fulfilled my responsibility. The moment I'm absolutely sure that I can back this up, I'm going on the air with it."

"*What*? Now wait a minute!" Higgins said. "Are you nuts? What the hell are you trying to do, start a citywide panic?"

"The people have a right to know—"

"Come off it! This is crazy! You try to pull anything like that, and so help me, I'll have you placed under arrest so fast your head will spin!"

"Go ahead and try it. But if I were you, I'd be more worried about your buddy, Cord. He's the one with his finger on the button."

She hung up.

Higgins stared at the speakerphone. The woman had gone completely around the bend. If she went on the air with a crazy story like that. . . . Only what if it *wasn't* crazy? No, thought Higgins, dismissing the possibility as ludicrous. But then, Linda Tellerman had never been someone to go off half-cocked. She was a good reporter. A pain in the ass, but he had to admit that she was damn good at her job and she wasn't irresponsible. And then he remembered something that Zach Cord used to say back in the old days, when he'd get fed up with the bureaucrats.

"*If they had any goddamn sense, they'd let the military handle things instead of running around like dogs chasing their own tails. We're the only ones who ever get anything done. If I had my way, I'd kick all those bastards out and put this country under martial law. Wipe out all the goddamn rebels, raiders and anarchists and get things fucking organized for Christ's sakes!"*

But back then, they'd all said things like that at one time or another. Just frustrated soldiers blowing off some steam, that's all it was.

Or was it?

Zach always was a maverick. He always did things his own way. He always got results, and his first loyalty was always to the people under his command. But this . . . this was really crazy. . . .

Higgins buzzed his secretary.

"Nancy? Get me Warren Air Force Base out in Wyoming. I want to speak to General Cord."

"Yes, sir, right away."

He took a deep breath. He'd hadn't spoken to Zach Cord in a long time. What would he say to him? Hi, Zach, how're you doin'? Long time. Listen, I hear you're planning to nuke us all here in New York. Any truth to that? Yeah, they'd probably have a good laugh over the whole thing. Several moments later, his secretary buzzed him back.

"Mr. Higgins, I've got Warren on the line."

He switched on the speakerphone.

"Zach! How the hell are you, you old bastard?"

"This is Lt. Grogan, Officer of the Day speaking."

"I asked for General Cord," said Higgins. "My secretary didn't tell you who was calling?"

"She did that, sir, but General Cord is a very busy man. He's not taking any calls right now. What can I do for you?"

"You can get on the horn to General Cord, Lieutenant, and tell him that Oliver Higgins of the CIA is calling."

"I'm sorry, sir, I can't do that. As I've already explained—"

"Now you listen to me, shavetail," Higgins said, "I knew Zachary Cord when you were still getting potty trained. We served together in the SOG. I sincerely suggest you pick up your phone and let him know who's calling, or by this time next week, you'll be a private shoveling manure in the most God-forsaken agro-commune I can find. You got me, Mister?"

There was a brief silence. "One moment, sir."

Higgins waited, annoyed. Fucking army Mickey Mouse, he

thought. After a short while, the OD came back on the phone.

"General Cord will speak to you, Mr. Higgins. One moment, please, I'll put you through."

A minute later, Cord was on the phone.

"Skeet? That really you?"

"It's me, Zach. It's been a long time. How are you?"

"Still eating bureaucrats like you for breakfast," Cord said, with a chuckle. "So you're still with the agency, huh? Gettin' fat behind a desk? What's on your mind?"

"Oh, just thought I'd call and ask you about this story that I heard," said Higgins.

"What story's that?"

Higgins chuckled. "It's about those missiles you're baby-sitting out there. I hear you've got them pointed at us here in New York."

There was a brief silence. Higgins felt a chill run down his spine.

"Where'd you hear that?" said Cord.

"A little bird told me."

"Yeah?" What else did that little bird tell you?"

Higgins swallowed hard. His stomach suddenly felt tense.

"Something about how you weren't dismantling any of those missiles out there. About how you were getting them all operational. About how you were keeping those scientists under guard and bringing in Delta Force and Rangers and putting the base on full alert while you were getting ready to pull off a military coup. Funny joke, huh?"

"That bird's name wouldn't happen to be Sgt. Reese Tracy, would it!"

"What if it would?"

"He's a goddamn traitor." There was slight pause. "You calling from New York, Skeet?"

Higgins moistened his lips. "Yeah. The Federal Building."

"You shoulda stuck with me, Skeet. Good soldier like you doesn't belong behind a desk. You should come out here. Open country. Lots of space. I could use a man like you. Put you to work, trim off that office fat. New York's not a healthy place to be."

"Zach . . . what are you telling me?"

"We go back a long way, Skeet. You saved my life once,

so I'll tell you this for old times' sake. Hang up the phone, pack your bags and get out of town."

He heard the click as Cord hung up the receiver.

Higgins stared at the speakerphone with stunned disbelief.

"Holy shit...." he whispered.

He buzzed his secretary.

"Nancy, this is top priority. Get me the President, right away!"

# 5

When Steele left the laboratory, he had no idea what had happened while he was in the isolation room. The walled-off cubicle doubled as an operating theatre and an observation chamber. It was where he had been programmed when they had completed the long and complicated series of procedures that had transformed him into a cyborg. His body had been hooked up to life support machinery until it was time to run the program that loaded his own mental engrams into his cybernetic brain. When he woke up, or more accurately, when he was brought on line, he had no memory of anything that had happened between the time that Victor Borodini's assassins had ambushed him and the time he came to in the project lab. This time, it was much different.

Instead of losing a large block of time out of his life, time in which he had become transformed into something that was both more and less than human, this time he remembered. He had regained memories that he had lost. Memories that had been taken from him.

When they had completed the repairs and the upgrading

procedures after his encounter with Stalker, he had come to feeling like an alcoholic who had gone on an extended drinking binge, a waking black-out during which he had done things he could not remember. Only, unlike a drunk in such a situation, Steele had awakened feeling fit and healthy. He simply had blanks in his memory that he could not account for.

He had remembered everything about his past, from his childhood right up to his adult life in the Strike Force. He remembered how he had become a cyborg and how he had fought the street gangs and taken down the Borodini Enclave, but he had no memories of his partner, Mick Taylor, and there had been no memories of his family. He had been partnered with Mick Taylor for five years. He had been married to Janice for a little over nineteen years. They had a son and daughter. And those memories had simply been removed, downloaded to computer storage and then erased from his engram matrix. It was terrifying that they could do something like that.

From the moment he had realized what he had become, Steele had clung tenaciously to the idea of his own humanity, but he had felt like a man scaling a rock wall, a climber whose pitons had pulled loose and whose line had broken, so that he was left clinging to a sheer stone cliff with nothing but his bleeding fingers. Below was a bottomless abyss. And his grip was slipping.

More than half of him was synthetic. Fusion powered, superstrong nysteel alloy and state-of-the-art microminiaturized electronic circuitry. But the rest of him was human, the same Donovan Steele that he had always been. His human cells still held the genetic template for who and what he was. His human heart still pumped real blood and his human lungs still breathed real air. His torso, from just below the waist up to his bionic optics, was still organic. The only exceptions were the nysteel ribcage, the articulated nysteel spinal reinforcement, the nysteel jaw and polymer/ceramic teeth, the tiny fusion generator implanted in his chest and the bullet-proof polymer skin grafts that covered him from his neck down to his abdominal area.

But his brain was a computer. A computer programmed with the information downloaded from his own organic brain and augmented with supplementary engram data. So what did that make him? Was he a man who was part machine or a machine that was part man? The difference, to him, was crucial. He could still make love to a woman and he was capable of fathering a child. That child would be human in every way, but would its father be a man or an ambulatory computer? And even if his brain was a computer programmed with his own identity, could a computer have a soul?

Those questions had plagued Steele right from the beginning. And as both his psychiatrist, Dr. Dev Cooper, and his priest, Father Liam Casey, had told him, there were no easy answers. There had never been a man with a computer for a brain before. The only answers that would do him any good were those that he would find within himself. And those answers were elusive. It was like trying to grab hold of quicksilver.

The only thing that enabled Steele to cling to his perception of his own humanity was the engram matrix he was programmed with. It was only that which enabled him to define himself *as* himself, the man that he had been before. It was the essence of his humanity. It was all he had.

He occasionally wondered what they had done with his organic brain once they had taken all the information from it and removed it, but they hadn't told him and he had never asked. He visualized some cybernetic surgeon dropping it unceremoniously into a plastic-lined garbage can. There were some who were convinced that at that moment, Donovan Steele had died. Legally, the courts had taken that position. Brain death equals legal death. A computer, regardless what it was programmed with, could have no civil rights. That was what the court had based its decision on when it had granted Janice her divorce. Steele always thought it was an odd sort of decision, since in a strictly legal sense, it meant that Janice had divorced a dead man.

But the fact was that he had never really died. His body had never ceased to function. His heart had not stopped beating and his lungs had not stopped breathing. And at no time had his brain function ever really ceased. It had simply been moved from one receptacle into another.

Janice had divorced him because she didn't want her children to have "some kind of robot" for a father. And, in granting her divorce, the court had also granted a restraining order, enjoining him from attempting to contact her or the kids in any way. He could have appealed it, but it would have taken years. It would have been the most controversial case in all of legal history, a case with implications so unsettling that no court would have been anxious to decide it. And there was simply no way he could afford it, nor had he wanted to drag his children through such a legal circus. Deep down inside, he hadn't been entirely convinced that Janice wasn't right. Only Jason and Cory had been convinced that she was wrong in doing what she did.

Janice had told them he had died, but they had soon found out the truth and Cory had run away from home. Jason had followed to look for her, only to discover that his sister had fallen victim to a savage pimp and been turned out as a prostitute. Now she was dead. Steele remembered it all now and the pain was like a hot knife in his gut. It burned with an incandescent agony. Cory's shame and degradation, followed by her violent death at the age of just fifteen; Jason's torment, anger and resentment; Janice's pain and guilt, transformed into a cold rage against himself; it all came back to him now. It washed over him like waves of sulphuric acid, eating away at his soul. This was what they had tried to spare him. Yet much as it hurt, he clung to those relentlessly agonizing memories, cherishing the pain, because it was all that he had left.

It would always be there now. The rigid control that both his willpower and his cybernetic brain endowed him with would enable him to compartmentalize those searing memories, to lock them away somewhere within the recesses of his computer mind until those times when he would be alone, in the privacy of his own reflections. And at such times, in the quiet, in the dark, he could summon up those memories and allow them to envelop him in gut-wrenching torment, because that was how Cory could live for him again. That was how Jason would always be with him, even though he might never see him again. And that was how his own humanity would survive, burning within him like the very fires of hell. It was an exquisite agony that he desperately needed, because he knew that a machine could never feel pain.

Those thoughts were foremost in his mind as he left the lab. He had no way of knowing that within moments after he left the building, numb with grief, Higgins was on the phone to the President of the United States. He had no way of knowing that some two thousand miles away, a young man's flight across the high plains of Colorado was setting him upon a path that would soon intersect with his. And he had no way of knowing that the memories that he had just regained had, at the same time, been accessed by another... a living electronic entity that was his own twin, a cybernetic doppelganger that had been desperately seeking the completion of its own identity and was even now suffering the same cruel torments that were mercilessly wracking him.

For a brief time, the two of them had experienced communion, and though Steele was unaware of it, the matrix clone had touched him and a bond was forged. For the matrix, as for Steele, the gaps had been filled in. And they were both complete. But for the matrix, the pain was even more unbearable, because there was no physical outlet for it. Unlike Steele, it could not experience that awful tightness in its chest or that aching, churning feeling in the pit of its stomach, because it had no body in which to experience the physical expression of emotional stress, the vital nervous sensations that served the cleansing function of release. Trapped as it was inside the electronic net, the matrix that was Steele's cybernetic twin could only assimilate his tragic memories and suffer from its inability to express the grief it shared with him.

And so it fled, hurtling through the power lines, as if trying to escape the source of all its pain, seeking something with which to blot it out. It sped through the building's phone lines, fastening upon snatches of other people's lives as their minutiae hummed over the wires. It heard a congressman arranging an assignation with his mistress over his private line. It eavesdropped on an aide leaking confidential information to a member of the press. It listened in on a secretary discussing sexual harassment in the office with one of her girlfriends. And there was no respite, no refuge to be found in the sordid, squalid little details it gleaned from other people's lives, all petty disillusionments and frustrations, shallow lusts and superficial hungers, irritations, passions and annoyances and....

"...absolutely certain about this, Mr. Higgins?"

"There's no question, Mr. President. I just spoke with General Cord. We served in SOG together and there was a time *when Zach and I were very close. And for the sake of that old friendship, he just warned me to pack my bags and get out of town."*

"He actually said that?"

*"Word for word. Sir, he's apparently gone far enough that he's got nothing to hide anymore. If the government won't accede to his demands, he can launch missiles from Warren Air Force Base and target New York, or Boston, or Chicago, or any other city that he chooses to make an example of. And he knows there's practically nothing we can do to stop him."*

"We're talking about taking on the government, and we can't even take out one lousy pickup truck with a helicopter gunship? Jesus fucking Christ!"

General Cord finished doing up the buttons on the blouse of his Cobra Force uniform. He had eight rows of ribbons over his breast pocket, souvenirs of his many campaigns. His black jump boots were spit-shined to a mirror-bright gloss, and his trousers were neatly pressed and bloused just so over his boots. On his belt, he wore an old 9mm. Beretta 92-F in a cordura flap holster. It was not a state-of-the-art polymer/ceramic weapon and its bluing was worn in places, but it had served him well throughout his long career and he was never without it. Col. Tyler stood before him in a position approximating parade rest, but even when he was at ease, Tyler looked as if he were standing at attention. Particularly in the presence of his commanding officer.

"I'm sorry, sir," he said. "Tracy will have reached Denver by now, but we've alerted the police there to be on the lookout for him. The Denver Strike Force has a complete description on him, and they've been told that he's unbalanced, armed and very dangerous."

"Forget about him," Cord said.

"Sir?"

"I said forget about him. If the Denver cops manage to find him before word gets out about what we're doing here, so much the better, but Tracy doesn't really matter anymore. We're better off without that traitor. I'm more concerned about the people we've got here. Where there was one Tracy, there could be others. The government may try to mount an operation against us. Tracy managed to get through to Oliver Higgins of the CIA. He's a good man, served with me in the SOG. He called me a little while ago, checking out what Tracy told him. I could've strung him along, but Higgins saved my life once, so I owed him something. Besides, there's not much point in trying to keep this a secret any longer. There isn't anything that they can do to stop us now. I gave Higgins fair warning. As far as I'm concerned, that squares all accounts between us. I gave him a chance to join us, but he made the wrong decision once before, when he turned down my offer to join the Cobra Force, and now he's about to make the wrong decision once again."

Cord shook his head sadly. "It's too bad. He was a good soldier, but he's gotten soft from all those years behind a desk. He's become a bureaucrat like all the rest of 'em. By now, he'll have spoken to the President, and they're probably scrambling around like chickens with their heads cut off, wondering what the hell to do."

"I don't see what they *can* do, sir," said Tyler. "You really think they'll try to hit us?"

"They can try," said Cord, "if they can manage to put together an assault force. But logistically, they're up shit creek without a paddle. I've been in touch with all the area commanders. A lot of them are just about as disgusted with the government as I am. Some of them came right out and promised their support, but I think most of them are just going to sit this one out on the sidelines, waiting to see if we can pull it off or not. I can't really blame them. They're being smart. But I have a feeling that if they receive any orders to mobilize, a whole lot of minor insurrections will occur throughout the country, pinning down their troops. Maybe we can't count on all of them to throw in with us right from the start, but they won't work against us, either. All Tracy's done is force us to move our timetable up a little. And that suits me just fine. I was getting tired of waiting."

He put on his Cobra Force beret and adjusted it, then checked his appearance in the full-length mirror. "All right, Colonel. Let's get this show on the road."

The troops were all assembled on the parade ground. With the exception of the Cobras, they were all unarmed and drawn up in company formation. The Cobras were formed in front of the parade stand. Tyler marched out to the stand and stood behind the microphone, which was hooked up to a portable PA system.

"TEN*hut*!"

Tyler took the role call, the stood aside for Cord.

"At ease," said Cord. He looked out at the troops. "Many of you people have probably had a lot of questions about what we're doing here at Warren. Officially, our mission here was to open up the silos and the LCFs and dismantle the remaining missiles, so that they wouldn't pose a threat to the security of this nation. However, the greatest threat this nation faces now is not from the Peacekeeper missile system, but from the fat and lazy bureaucrats in the government back east who have thus far failed to take appropriate measures to reunite this country."

Tyler watched the troops for their reaction. They were all listening attentively. The inefficiency of the bureaucrats back east was something they were familiar with.

"Make no mistake," said Cord, looking out at them. "We are at war. You have all, at one time or another, had to face the forces of anarchy that permeate this nation. You have all had to put your lives on the line, answering the call of duty often without pay and without proper supplies. You have all had the thankless task of fighting what amounts to little more than a holding action against the forces of lawlessness in this great land, and I am sure there have been times when you have all asked yourselves if those idiots back in Congress had the faintest idea of what in hell they were doing."

Tyler watched their faces. A lot of them were nodding. What Cord was saying struck home to every one of them. There wasn't a single soldier out there who hadn't felt, at one time or another, that what they were trying to do was like pissing in the wind.

"I've asked myself that question many times," continued Cord. "I've asked myself that question each time I've had to look at troops who had not been paid in months, who have had to put up with lack of proper food and clothing because the supply lines keep breaking down or because requisitions have been lost or stalled by endless bureaucratic red tape. I've asked myself what, if anything, we were supposed to be accomplishing. Because we don't seem to be accomplishing very much at all. It all comes down to lack of proper leadership. This country is in a state of anarchy, but the bureaucrats back east can't see past the borders of their cities. They're still clinging to the old system, because they *are* the old system, and they can't see, or they refuse to see, that the old system's broken down."

Cord stood at ease, a loose version of the position of parade rest, his hands clasped behind him, his legs spread about shoulder-width apart, his head erect, his upper body turning slightly as he looked first at one company, then at another, making eye contact with individual soldiers, pausing here and there for emphasis. He had charisma and he was a persuasive and articulate speaker. The things that he was saying echoed the thoughts that many of them had.

"Politicians are not qualified to fight a war," he said. "That's a job for soldiers. But soldiers can't fight when their hands are tied by politicians. Throughout history, soldiers have died needlessly because of the ignorance and folly of bureaucrats. And what have their ignorance and folly brought us to? A country disunited, torn by civil strife and lawlessness, plagued with disease and shortages of every kind. Towns at the mercy of outlaw gangs and raiders, cities surrounded by ghettos that are war zones. And I have had to ask myself, can I, as a soldier and a patriot, as a man who loves this country and would gladly die for it, allow this chaos to continue?"

He paused for effect, as if were asking *them* the question.

"The answer is that I cannot," he said. "We now have within our grasp an opportunity to correct all the mistakes of the past few decades, a chance to set this nation back upon the path to greatness! A chance to pull this country back together! It is a chance that no man can pass up and still call himself a patriot. We have a formidable task ahead of us. It is a task that will require boldness, courage and resolve. A task that will require selflessness and dedication. A task that will require some very hard decisions, but those decisions *must* be made if we are to bring this nation back from the brink of oblivion."

He paused once again, as if weighing the gravity of those decisions. The silence was profound. There was no foot shuffling or coughing. They were all hanging on his every word.

"Several thousand years ago," said Cord, "when Julius Caesar led the legendary legions of ancient Rome, he would stand before them on the eve of battle, much as I stand before you now, and he would speak to them forthrightly, with an open heart, and tell them of the trials that lay ahead. He would tell them, as I am telling you, that he had faith in them, trust in their courage and ability, and that when the time came for them to march, he would take pride in being with them in the vanguard, with sword and shield in hand, risking his own life in the heat of battle as a commander should, fighting alongside the men he loved, fighting for the principles and values that they all held dear. And when those principles and values were about to be subverted by the corrupt politicians of the Roman Senate who would have let the empire fall rather than give up their decadent and selfish pleasures, Caesar marched his legions against Rome itself, to save the empire from those who would destroy it from within!"

Nice touch, thought Tyler. Effective. He smiled to himself. The Old Man really knew how to work a crowd.

"Throughout the centuries," Cord continued, "it has always been the soldiers who have carried aloft the torch of freedom. Throughout the long and glorious annals of military history, it was always the soldiers who were asked to make the sacrifices, to lay down their lives if necessary so that others could be free. That torch has now been passed to us. And it is our responsibility to see that torch burn brightly, so that it can never be extinguished! We must shoulder that responsibility. We must be steadfast and resolute. We cannot fail the test, for the future of this great country has been placed within our hands. Together, we must stand, shoulder to shoulder, and fight for that which we believe in. For our future and the future of our loved ones. For the future of our children and the generations yet to come.

"Today," said Cord, his voice rising, "we cross the Rubicon! Today, we take upon ourselves the task for which all of us were trained! Today, we take up the burden that the corrupt and selfish bureaucrats have allowed to slip from their shoulders! Today, we make a new beginning! And someday, you will all be able to tell your grandchildren that you were there to play a part when this great country was reborn, to rise up from the ashes like the legendary Phoenix, spreading its golden wings across the land!"

Here it comes, thought Tyler.

"Today," said Cord, "I am declaring this country placed under martial law! Henceforth, Warren Air Force Base will become the temporary seat of government of the United States of America, and together we will take up the task of rebuilding this great nation!"

Tyler saw the shocked expressions of amazement on many of their faces. He tensed. The whole thing rested on the Old Man, on his leadership ability and on the dissatisfaction of the troops, many of whom hadn't even had a decent uniform until they had been transferred in. The Cobra Force would support him to a man, as would the elite troops who were recently brought in, but many of these people had never served under him in combat. They had never had the opportunity to form that intense bond of personal allegiance that came with going into action led by a man like Cord. The Old Man was a living legend, but would his fame and reputation be enough to gain their loyal support in a military coup?

"From our headquarters here," said Cord, "I will be in constant touch with the other units of our Armed Forces. Our first priority will be a massive reorganization effort. We will establish a dependable network of supply lines and communication. We will establish a military tribunal that will dictate policy to the legislative branch, and we will take over the administration of the agro-communes and the industrial centers. Police and Strike Force units in urban areas will be brought under military supervision and assigned military advisors to oversee tactics and training. We will institute a system of impressment, administered by the military, with every able-bodied male and female over the age of sixteen required to serve a period of at least six years in the police or the Armed Forces. In this manner, we will open up new career opportunities for the disenfranchised citizens forced to struggle for survival in the urban ghettos and the poverty-stricken towns and settlements, harnessing the energy of our younger generation and giving them the chance to make a difference in the future of this country. We will insure that all troops receive proper supplies and regular pay, with bonuses for hazardous duty. We will institute a system of work farms for the criminal classes that will teach them a trade and make them productive members of society even while incarcerated."

As the Old Man outlined the basic steps of his program, Tyler watched the faces of the troops intently and he saw that it was going over. They were smiling and nodding to each other. What Cord was telling them was making sense. But some of them were still listening with expressions of shocked disbelief. And Cord's next words had a sobering effect.

"I spoke a little while ago about the necessity of making some very hard decisions. The time has come for us to look at those decisions in the harsh light of reality." He paused. "At such a time, the responsibility of command weighs heavily upon my shoulders. A commander must concern himself not only with the success of achieving his objective, but with the price that must be paid in achieving that success."

He paused again, looking out at all of them, allowing his words to sink in.

"The people who are currently in power in this country have their own vested interests to protect. They will not easily surrender their authority. They will not easily give up the perks of leadership and power. I spoke before of Caesar and of the grave decision that he had to make when he chose to march his legions against Rome. It is a dark day when a soldier must decide to throw off the repressive authority of his superiors and take matters into his own hands for the greater good of the nation. Like you, I am but a soldier, sworn to do his duty to protect democracy. I have no desire to be a Caesar. I have no desire to set myself up as a military dictator. I have no desire to see our great nation reduced to a totalitarian regime. Throughout my life, I have always been proud to be a part of that great tradition of service in support of the Constitution of this free land of ours. But these are times of desperation. And desperate times call for desperate measures. Never in the history of this great land have we been faced with such a trial. Never have freedom and democracy been so sorely tested.

"I ask you," Cord continued, "is it democracy when our elected representatives vote generous pay raises for themselves each year, while the men and women who serve in our Armed

Forces are reduced to food rationing and wearing threadbare uniforms? Is it democracy when the members of our legislature live in pampered luxury, insulated from the poverty that's all around them, while the people whom they claim to represent must bear the heavy burden of usurious taxation, unable to buy even the bare necessities because of the high rate of inflation and the instability of the economy? If all men are, indeed, created equal, with a right to life, and liberty, and the pursuit of happiness, then why do the bureaucrats live in spacious penthouses, surrounded by armed guards, while so many of our citizens are homeless, starving, and ridden with disease? Are any of us really free so long as *even one man* must live in chains?''

Cord's voice rose and trembled in anger and righteous indignation. He held his arms out to the troops, in supplication.

"I ask you, do you share my rage against the injustice in this land? Let me hear you! Can we afford to continue on our present course?"

The answer came back in a resounding chorus: "No!"

"Then you have given me my mandate," Cord said. "But those who have grown fat at the expense of others will oppose us. We must be strong, and united in our purpose. As I stand here before you today, I am filled with pride at being able to lead you wonderful people in our crusade—and yes, it is a holy task—to reunite this beleagured nation! Fate has brought us to this place and we must now seize the initiative! Out there, on the desert plains, standing in their silos like grim and terrible juggernauts, are the weapons that almost brought our great civilization to an end. The decision to employ those dreadful weapons in the Bio War came not from any soldier, but from the bureaucrats who sought desperately to protect their power. And now, ironically, those very same weapons can help us forge a new beginning!''

He paused and the silence was a palpable thing. Cord took a deep breath and let it out slowly.

"I spoke of hard decisions, and this may be the hardest one that any soldier has ever had to make. When the first atomic bomb was exploded on Hiroshima, it brought about a devastating loss of life, unrivaled in all of history until the dark day that the Bio War began. And yet, the lesson of that grim and terrible act was not lost. It brought about the end of World War II, and yes, the cost was great, but it would have been far greater had that war continued. We face a similar grave decision now. Yet, in a sense, the decision is really not ours to make."

Tyler noted the subtle manner in which Cord was including them all in the enterprise by using words like "we" and "our" instead of "me" and "mine." He was a naturally gifted public speaker, and his words were having a telling effect.

"The bureaucrats back east have failed in their responsibility," Cord said. "Now it is up to us. We must take the initiative. We must convince them of our resolve. And if they try to call our bluff... we must *prove* to them that we're not bluffing! What's at stake is the future of this country. Our future and the future of our children. I'd like for us to leave them a better world than the one we were born into. History will judge our actions. And, for the sake of history, for the sake of this great land of ours, for the sake of the children and the generations yet to come, *we—must—not—falter*!

"I'd like to ask you all to join me in a moment of prayer," Cord said. He bowed his head. "Almighty God... we stand gathered here before you, humbled on this historic day by the great task that lies before us. We ask your blessing in our enterprise, we pray for courage, purpose and resolve. We pray that we will not be forced to use the terrible sword which you have given unto us this day, but should we be left no other choice, we pray for understanding and forgiveness, and we pray for guidance in binding up this country's wounds."

He looked out at the troops. "And now, I would like to ask you all to bow your heads and pray aloud with me. Our Father, who art in Heaven, hallowed by thy name. Thy kingdom come ... thy will be done...."

Corporal Pat Summers was not praying. She stood in her place in formation, her head bowed along with all the others, listening to the soldiers around her speaking the words of The Lord's Prayer, but she was numb with shock. Tracy had been right. Cord was going to use the missiles! There had been scuttlebutt about that all over the base for the past few weeks, vague rumors about some sort of secret orders to get the network active for national defense, but no one had ever actually considered that Cord might use them to support a military coup! She stood, stunned, as she heard the soldiers praying all around her and wondered if it was possible that she was the only one who hadn't lost her senses. She wanted to break out of formation and run, flee from this madness, but there wasn't anywhere to run to. There wasn't anything that anyone could do. Either the government back east would succumb to Cord's authority, or he would nuke them. And there was no defense. None whatsoever.

She had no relatives back east. In fact, she now remembered the personnel forms she'd been asked to fill out prior to being transferred in. She had to fill out where she was born and list all the places she had lived. There had also been a question asking her to list all living relatives, who they were, what their relationship was, and where they were currently residing. And, now that she thought of it, she realized that since she'd been at Warren, she hadn't met anyone at all from back east, or anyone who'd spoken about having any people there. At the time she had filled out the forms, she had thought it was simply more pointless Mickey Mouse. Now she understood.

And she realized that Cord would make it work. He had to have been planning this for months, maybe even years. He had to have discreetly sounded out other area commanders, to see if they would support him. And even if they wouldn't, what could they possibly do? They didn't need all the missiles operational. They needed only a few of them, hell, even one would do. And even if the government could mount some sort of an assault against the base, there was simply no way they could prevent the missiles being launched. Cord had them exactly where he wanted them. They would have to see that any resistance would be fruitless. They would capitulate. They'd have to.

Only what would happen if they wouldn't?

*"And if they try to call our bluff . . . we must prove to them that we're not bluffing. . . ."*

Oh, God, she thought. I can't be a part of this. I can't. Please, God, I can't. . . .

She knew now why Tracy had gone AWOL. And she wished that he had told her, so that she could have gone with him.

Somehow, some way, she had to get out of here. Only where could she go? What would she do?

Maybe it would all work out for the best, she thought, clutching at straws. Maybe they wouldn't call Cord's bluff. They knew his reputation. They knew that Cord had never backed down from anything or anyone. Maybe they'd capitulate and maybe Cord would actually pull it off, get the military behind him and accomplish everything he said he'd do. Reunite the country. Get it back upon its feet once more. Maybe it would really work. She wanted to believe that very much. She tried hard to make herself believe it. The bureaucrats back east had really made a mess of things. They were just stupid enough to make a mess of this, as well.

She glanced up out of the corners of her eyes at the soldiers all around her as they prayed, looking for some sign that she was not alone in the panic she was feeling, but if any of them felt the same, she saw no indication of it. It seemed that Cord had convinced them all. He had promised them the moon and he would deliver it, even if it meant shattering the earth. He had them on his side. He had the Cobras, he had missiles, he had it all.

God help us, she thought.

"... and lead us not into temptation, but deliver us from evil ... for thine is the kingdom ... and the power ... and the glory ... forever and ever. ... Amen."

# 6

The waiter brought them their drinks and asked if they would like to order. He shook his head and said, "Nothing for me, thanks." The waiter looked at Donna and she shook her head. The waiter left and they sat for a moment in silence. It was getting late, and all around them, couples sat in the cozy little booths and at small tables covered with red and white checkered cloths. Each table had an empty, green glass wine bottle on it with a candle stuck into the end. Reproductions of old movie posters hung framed upon the rough, unpainted brick walls. They sat beneath a poster of Humphrey Bogart and Ingrid Bergman, cheek to cheek, with the legend *Casablanca* printed in red script underneath. A Warner Brothers, First National Films, Inc. release, with Paul Henreid, Claude Rains and Sidney Greenstreet. Directed by Michael Curtiz.

Donna was staring down into her drink. She hadn't touched it. She looked up at him and brushed her long black hair away from her face. She swallowed hard and moistened her lips.

"You're leaving me, aren't you?" she said softly.

She'd beaten him to the punch. His well-rehearsed little

speech went right out the window. He had gone over and over it in his mind during the last few days, trying to find exactly the right way to tell her, but as usual, she had known what he was thinking, so he simply nodded. He had to look away from her. He couldn't face that stricken expression in her eyes. It was too much. God, why did it have to be so hard?

"I knew it," she said softly, looking down at the table again. "I had a feeling this was coming, and when you didn't come home last night, I knew it for sure." She paused briefly. "When you called, I thought you were going to tell me over the phone." Her mouth twitched in a slight grimace that tried to be a smile, but didn't quite make it. "I'd like to thank you for doing it face to face. At least that's something."

He sighed. "Donna . . . I've been trying very hard to find a way to—"

"No," she said with an abrupt shake of her head. "Don't. Don't try to find a way to soften it. It can't be done. It hurts, Jonathan. There's no way that you can make it not hurt. But you don't have to worry. I won't make a scene. I . . ." her voice caught and she took a deep breath. "I may cry a little . . . and later on, I'll probably cry a lot . . . but I'll try not to embarrass you in public. I know how much you hate that."

"That isn't why I asked you to meet me here," he said awkwardly, knowing it was a bold-faced lie. That was exactly why.

She looked up again, her eyes moist, and glanced around the small cafe. "It was almost seven years ago," she said in a vague, detached sort of tone. "Next week, it would have been seven years exactly." Her gaze settled on a small booth in the corner. A young couple sat there now, holding hands across the table. "It was that booth right over there. Remember?"

He shut his eyes. Jesus Christ. What a goddamn fool. He had forgotten. He had actually forgotten. They'd been here so many times over the years, it had completely slipped his mind that this was where he had proposed to her. How could he have forgotten something like that? They always used to come here, and when he called, it was simply the first place that came to mind. . . . Oh, shit. Damn, damn, *damn*!

"Is there someone else?" she asked, still looking vaguely at the young couple at "their" table.

He shook his head. "No. There's no one."

She nodded and looked back at him, then quickly averted her gaze, looking back down at her still untouched drink.

"I suppose I'd better have some of this," she said, taking a swallow. She took another, then another. "I think I may get drunk tonight."

"Donna... I tried. I really tried, but—"

"*Don't*. For God's sake, don't try to make excuses. We've always been honest with each other. Well... almost always, anyway. Trudy was one of your rare exceptions."

He stared at her, stunned. "You knew?"

She smiled sadly. "Of course, I knew."

"How? Christ, she actually *told* you?"

Donna made a little sound that was halfway between a chuckle and a snort. A brief, sharp expulsion of breath. She was turning the glass, almost empty now, around and around between her cupped hands.

"No, she didn't tell me. She'd never have done that. But I know my little sister." Her lips compressed into a tight grimace. "We've always had a sort of one-sided sibling rivalry. It didn't matter what it was, if it was mine, she wanted it. And sooner or later, she always found a way to get it. Like she got you."

"Why didn't you say anything?"

She shrugged. "What was I supposed to say. Stop fucking my little sister?" She shook her head. "No, I knew it was nothing but a fling for you. And a way for her to spite me behind my back, the way she always did. She was young and pretty, with a terrific body and the morals of an alley cat.... Anyway, it doesn't matter now." She shrugged. "Oh, I was hurt and I was bitter, but I didn't really blame you for wanting her. She's eminently wantable. And at least you had the decency to be discreet about it."

"I... I don't know what to say. I'm—"

"For God's sake, just don't say you're sorry. Don't say you didn't mean it. At least spare me that indignity."

He burned with shame. There was nothing left to say. Nothing at all. He wanted desperately to just get up and leave, just walk away and end it, but it couldn't be that easy. There was simply too much pain. He couldn't even look at her anymore. They had buried their marriage when they had buried their three children. They had stood there together, mute with grief, staring at the three little hermetically sealed urns—the law specified cremation for all victims of Virus 3—and all he had been able to think about was how they had taken them to their deaths.

The twins had already started manifesting signs of the disease by the time they reached the hospital, and it had taken four orderlies, masked and dressed in heavily padded clothing to protect against a bite, like attack dog trainers, to drag them off into a little room, and they weren't even allowed to watch as the lethal injections were administered. Donna had become hysterical, and it had been necessary for them to physically tear her away from Janey, whose face had started to break out in the awful running sores, and her frenzied screams of "Mommy! Mommy" were the last things that he heard.

He had felt arms upon him, and a needle being plunged into his vein, and for a moment he had thought that they had made a terrible mistake and were putting him to sleep as well, but it had only been a powerful, fast-acting sedative, to literally put him to sleep, and he had sagged in their arms, hearing the diminishing cries of his daughter as they dragged her down the hall and his wife's hysterical screams, and then he went numb and it all faded away. His consciousness, their marriage, everything.

It had been necessary for Donna to remain in the hospital. When he awoke, they told him she had had a nervous breakdown. He had asked to see her, but they told him, as kindly as they could, that it would be impossible. He had protested, but they told him that she didn't *want* to see him. He had demanded to see the doctor, and the doctor had taken him into his office and explained that, under the circumstances, he really could not allow him to see Donna. He explained about what happens when a person experiences complete nervous collapse, and he explained that what they had to concern themselves with now was allowing her to get better. It was not unusual, he said, for such a reaction to occur. She had been severely traumatized and she really wasn't thinking rationally.

She had placed the blame on him, for bringing the children there to die, and she simply couldn't bear the thought of seeing him. The doctor had explained that there was really nothing anyone could have done. There was no cure for Virus 3. At least, this way, the children had been spared a slow and agonizing death as screamers. It had been, under the circumstances, the kindest thing to do, and under the law, there had been no other choice. But Donna didn't understand that. In time, the doctor said, she would get over it and she would come to understand, but right now, she needed time to heal. She needed treatment. He hoped that he would understand.

He had understood, all right. The children had died, tragically, horribly, and she had left him to face it all alone. To bear the guilt and suffer all the pain. Alone.

After she had finally gotten out of the hospital, he had tried to tell himself that it would be all right, that the worst was over. That he could forgive her.

But he had found that he could not.

"I suppose there's nothing I can say to make you change your mind," she said.

He stared down at the table and shook his head.

"Well... I suppose that's it, then."

He said nothing.

"I love you," she said, her voice barely above a whisper.

He got up and threw some money down on the table.

"Goodbye, Donna."

"Jonathan... don't go!"

There was a sudden note of hysteria in her voice.

"Donna, please... you said you wouldn't make a scene...."

"I love you!"

He turned and started to walk away.

"I'm sorry. *Please... don't go!*"

People were turning to stare in his direction as he hurried out of the cafe.

"Steele! Come back! *Steele!*"

He bolted for the door.

"Steele! *Steele!*"

He awoke with a gasp in the darkness of his bedroom, covered with sweat.

*"Steele... Steele...."*

Raven sat up in bed beside him.

*"Steele... come back, Steele...."*

"Steele!" she said. "Honey, what is it? Another dream?"

*"Steele... this is Higgins.... Come back to project headquarters immediately... Steele... come back...."*

"It's Higgins," he said, getting out of bed. "He's calling on the broadcast link. Something's come up. I've got to get over there."

He started to get dressed.

"Honey, you don't look so good," she said. "Are you all right?"

No, he thought, I'm not all right. The ghosts are haunting me again. Another nightmare about Donna, the woman who was my wife, yet not my wife, a woman I had hurt, even though I'd never even met her. Jonathan, damn you for a son of a bitch, whoever the fuck you are, get the hell out of my mind!

"Yeah," he said, lying. "I'll be fine. Go back to sleep."

*"Steele to Higgins,"* he thought, mentally tying into the link. *"I'm receiving you. I'm on my way."*

East Colfax Avenue in Denver was a strange place. Coming from the east, it led through the town of Aurora, Colorado, down to the Capitol Hill district, where the gold dome of the capitol building gleamed brightly in the sunlight. In the distance, to the west, the foothills of the front range of the Rockies rose up majestically over the city's skyline. Once the red-light strip of Denver, East Colfax Avenue had experienced urban renewal in the days before the war. Police had swept the hookers from the streets; the porno theaters, strip joints and adult bookstores had been closed, and the buildings had been renovated to house bookstores, import shops, art galleries and fern bars.

Aurora had grown quickly and dramatically, exploding in a building boom as a bedroom community to house Denver commuters. But now, years after the war, Aurora was a no-man's-land, a surreal ghost town consisting of acres upon acres of largely deserted and dilapidated tract housing and condominiums with names like "Crestview Pines" and "Seaview Harbor," though there wasn't a pine tree or an ocean in sight. Gangs controlled the turf now, a mixture of Anglos, Hispanics and blacks, who differed from their eastern cousins in their western-influenced, piratical dress; seedy swashbucklers on motorcycles and horseback who rode the cracked and pot-holed suburban streets like hordes of cowboy Mongols, rustling cattle from the ranch enclaves on the plains and making fortresses out of the crackerbox townhouse apartment complexes.

At the time shortly before the war, Denver had grown so dramatically that unbroken development stretched from close to Fort Collins in the north almost to Colorado Springs in the south, but the war had changed all that. Colorado Springs was now a massive hot spot, devoid of life from missile strikes aimed at its technological centers and the NORAD complex in Cheyenne Mountain. Anything south of Castle Rock was unsafe, down to and including Pueblo, almost as far south as Walsenburg. The road down to Denver from Cheyenne skirted several hot spots and most of the area from Fort Collins down to Longmont was now deserted, with the exception of a small, yet powerful libertarian survivalist enclave in the picturesque town of Estes Park.

The largest settlement between Cheyenne and Denver could be found in Boulder, with its long history of idiosyncratic, counterculture sensibility. Nestled in a lovely valley, Boulder had become a haven for a number of bizarre religious cults that remained completely isolated from what was left of mainstream society. Not even the gangs in Denver's no-man's-land or the nomadic bands of raiders in the devastated countryside ventured anywhere near Boulder. It was just too weird to contemplate. It had a tendency to swallow people up.

In this part of the country, modern civilization had its bastion in Denver. Like New York's Midtown, the downtown area of Denver was the urban core city, with most of its economy centered in the district. The streets were relatively safe, except during the late hours of the night, when the gangs from no-man's-land often conducted guerrilla sorties into town, and the atmosphere in the city streets became reminiscent of Saigon during the Tet Offensive. And the farther one went from the Downtown core district, the less safe it became.

Sin had once again reclaimed East Colfax. Hookers choked

the avenue, selling the one commodity that has never been in short supply. Cheap motels dotted the far end of the strip, nearest the Aurora no-man's-land, while closer to the Capitol Hill District, there was a profusion of saloons, whorehouses and gambling arcades. It was a sort of DMZ buffer zone between the core city and no-man's-land, a loosely regulated combat zone with its streets patrolled by the Denver Strike Force, though they generally didn't give a damn about whatever went on inside the numerous questionable establishments along the strip. So long as gunfire did not spill out into the streets with too much regularity, the Denver Strike Force more or less pursued a policy of containment.

Reese Tracy sat behind a table in a small booth near the back of the Crazy Horse Club, which was located on the East Colfax Strip, roughly midway between the Capitol Hill District and the western border of the Aurora no-man's-land. He sat with his back against the wall, facing the front door at the far end of the dimly lit saloon. The saloon was laid out in a rectangular shape, with the bar running along the front, just inside the door. At the far end of the bar, on the side opposite the small entrance lobby, there was a flight of stairs leading up to a sort of catwalk that ran all around the club, about eight feet below the ceiling. This catwalk led behind and above the bar, around to the left side of the club, where there was another flight of stairs leading down to a small stage, ringed by a narrow apron upon which patrons could place their drinks, with chairs placed all around it. The catwalk continued on toward the back end of the club, where another long flight of stairs descended to yet another stage, this one with a small runway extending for a short distance out into the club, and from the back of that stage, there was a narrow walkway running along the wall, above the booths, to a third stage opposite the one on the left side of the club. Three stages in all, with the bartop comprising a fourth, on which scantily clad young women danced, moving from one stage to the next via the catwalk and the stairs, each of them dancing three numbers on each stage, making a circuit all around the club until they took their breaks and started moving among the tables, hustling the customers for drinks and tips and whatever else they might consider.

There were several burly-looking bouncers keeping an eye

on things from up on the catwalk, others stationed here and there throughout the club, all carrying sidearms and billy clubs. The dim illumination in the room was augmented by flashing lights and strobes, and the music throbbed loudly with a relentless beat, orchestrated by the female disc jockey in a glass booth above the bar. As the dancers moved from stage to stage, descending slowly and seductively down the flights of stairs, the D.J. identified them for the patrons over the PA system.

"On stage number one, we have *Tawny*, dancing for your pleasure! On stage number two, the sleek and sexy *Destiny*! On stage number three, get ready guys, here comes *Sabrina*! And down here below me on the bar—watch your drinks, guys, she gets a little carried away sometimes—go get 'em, *Stormy*! Come on, guys, put your hands together for these girls! And be sure to ask your favorite for a private table dance! If you like what you see, don't be shy, these girls are friendly. Boy, are they ever friendly! We had three of them get pregnant last month! Come on, people, let's hear some *noise* down there!"

A young waitress in a short black leather skirt, gold halter top and cowboy boots came over to ask Tracy if he wanted another drink.

"Another coffee, please," he said. "And could you bring me another pack of cigarettes?"

"Sure thing, hon. Comin' right up."

She left to bring his order, and he sat back against the cushions of the booth, taking a deep breath to steady his nerves. The coffee wasn't helping his nerves any, but it was keeping him awake, as were the cigarettes, which he was chain-smoking, though he was paying three times as much for them as he would have for the most expensive drink in the club. From where he was sitting, he could see the entire room.

On the stage to his left, a hard-looking, sultry black girl wearing nothing but spike heels and a G-string was bending over a group of men seated below her. Her back to them, she was looking at them coyly through her legs, running her fingers along the insides of her thighs. The men were staring intently at her barely covered crotch. On another stage, a voluptuous brunette was crouching down before a patron who was offering her a tip. She inched out across the apron, her legs spread on either side of him, and rolled the bill up into a small tube, which she placed between his teeth. Then she slid forward a little more, so that his face was inches from her crotch, and as she wrapped her legs around his head, she pulled the front of her G-string out, allowing him to deposit the bill inside. It must have been a decent tip, thought Tracy wryly, because she allowed him to root around in there for about five seconds before she moved away from him, gave him a smile and a brief kiss on the cheek, then got up and resumed her pelvic gyrations.

Tracy glanced at his watch. A half hour had passed since Linda Tellerman had told him she would call him back. He had no money when he arrived in Denver, so against his better judgment, he had hocked his battle helmet and his backpack, with one remaining rocket. The pawnbroker's eyes had lit up when he saw it, and he had instantly made the obvious deduction that Tracy was a deserter. He had tried to offer him a ludicrously low sum, but after a little irritable dickering, Tracy had lost his temper and raised his battle rifle, pulling back the bolt, and made the pawnbroker empty out his register. But just so he wouldn't feel like a thief, he had left the battle helmet and the backpack with the pawnbroker, knowing that the man could easily get a small fortune for them. He should have thought to have the man empty out his safe as well, but he had to draw the line somewhere. At least he now had about six hundred dollars in his pocket, which was nowhere near what the equipment had been worth, but what the hell, it hadn't cost him anything. And he still had his armor, his battle rifle and his 9mm.

When he had entered the club, the bouncers eyes had grown wide at the sight of the battle rifle and the 9mm. on his hip, and they had tried to tell him that he had to "check them" at the door. But Tracy had known that if he had done that, he'd never have seen them again. He simply told them that he didn't want any trouble, that he was on a little R and R from a special courier assignment in Downtown, and, he added in a level tone, if they wouldn't let him come in with his weapons, he just might come back with "a few of the boys in Cobra Force" and they would discuss it further. End of discussion. They had even waived the cover charge.

"Anything for our boys in the service."

## JAGGED STEELE    111

Just the same, several of the bouncers had taken up positions on the catwalk above him, where they could have a clear shot if he decided to get rowdy. He paid scant attention to them. He had no intention of getting rowdy. He was too damn tired. After a while, seeing that he wasn't making any trouble, they lost interest in him.

He had called Linda from the phone in the back of the club, by the restrooms. She had told him that she had passed his information on to the appropriate authorities and that she had spoken directly with a man named Oliver Higgins of the CIA.

"Did he believe you?" Tracy had asked.

"Let's say he was skeptical," she said, "but he's going to check it out. He wanted you to call him. He gave me a number where you can reach him, but I told him that I'd warn you about a possible trace. I think you should talk to him, Tracy. But be careful."

"I'll think about it," he said. "But I'd rather talk to you. Are you going to break the story?"

"I still haven't been able to fully substantiate it," she said, "but so far, everything you told me has checked out. Don't get me wrong, Tracy, it isn't that I don't believe you. My instincts tell me I can trust you, but I've got to have more than that before I go on the air with something like this. If this isn't on the level, then I could start a panic and that would be the end of my career."

He snorted. "Your *career*? You've gotta be kidding me! It isn't your career we're talking about, Miss Tellerman, it's your goddamn *life*! *Thousands* of lives are at stake here! For God's sake, what's it going to take for you to realize that?"

"Where are you calling from, Tracy?"

"I . . . I'm not sure it would be a very good idea to tell you. No offense, but—"

"You're calling from some bar in Denver. I can hear music in the background. Listen, have you got any money?"

"Some. But I'm not sure how long it's going to last. I really have no idea what to do. I don't know where I'm going from here—"

"Tracy, listen to me. I can try to get some people to help you. I can make a call to some people I know at our affiliate station in Denver. They're news people, Tracy, they're not going to turn you over to the police. Do you have a place to stay yet?"

"No, but—"

"Let me call them. Let me tell them what's going on. Believe me, Tracy, the news media's not going to sell you out. We just don't work that way. And if this story's on the level, they'll give you a chance to tell it. They'll put you on the air and you can tell the whole thing in your own words. I can get you some protection, Tracy, but you're going to have to cooperate with me. You're asking me to take an awful lot on trust. Okay, then. I'll trust you. I'll go on the air with this story tonight, but only if I get your complete cooperation. You're not the only one who's taking risks here. So what's it gonna be?"

He took a deep breath and thought about it for a moment.

"Tracy? You still there?"

"Yeah, I'm still here. All right. I'll take a chance on you, Miss Tellerman."

"Good boy. Call me Linda."

"Okay, Linda. I'm calling from the Crazy Horse Club in Denver." He gave her the number. "When you call back . . . ask for . . . uh . . . Trace Richards. I'll have them page me. But if I don't hear from you in an hour, I'm outta here."

"Okay, Tracy. Sit tight. I'll call you back as soon as I can set something up."

That had been almost an hour and a half ago and she still hadn't called back. Tracy's nerves were raw. Could she have sold him out? He wasn't certain what to do. Part of him wanted to get the hell away from there, find somewhere to hole up and then . . . then what? He didn't know. And part of him was afraid that if he got up to leave, she'd call back the moment he walked out the door. He didn't know what to do.

"Hey, soldier, got somethin' on your mind?"

He looked up to see a very pretty, slender, blue-eyed blond of about nineteen or twenty standing by his table. She had short hair, cut in a shag, and she was wearing high-heeled, short black boots and a curious sort of arrangement that consisted of a few strategically placed strips of black leather held together with small metal rings that displayed a lot of skin. He couldn't for the life of him figure out how she got it on or off, but there must have been a trick to it, because shedding your garments smoothly in a place like this was essential to the job.

"What?" he said.

"I've been working my ass off up there on the stage, trying to get your attention, and you haven't even looked at me once. Makes a girl feel sorta insecure, you know?"

"Oh. I'm sorry. Look, it's nothing personal . . . it's like you said, I've got a lot on my mind."

"Mind if I sit down and join you? I could sure use a break. These heels are killing me."

"Uh . . . sure, I guess."

She slipped into the booth and scooted up close beside him.

"You drinkin' coffee? Want anything stronger?"

"No, this is fine, thanks."

She waved the waitress over. "Another cup of coffee for the soldier here." She glanced at him. "Buy a girl a drink?"

"Yeah, sure, why not?"

"Scotch and soda," she said to the waitress. She looked back to him. She was sitting very close with her bare leg up against his. "My name's Stormy. What's yours?"

"Tracy," he answered, without thinking, then glanced at her nervously.

"You want to talk about it, hon?"

Tracy sighed. "No, not really." He grimaced. "I'm sorry. I don't mean to be rude. I guess I'm not very good company right now. I wouldn't mind if you went to another table."

"Hey, no, it's okay. You just sorta looked down in the dumps sitting here and I thought maybe I could come over and cheer you up." She put her arm around him and gently rubbed his shoulder. "God, you're tense! Come on, honey, loosen up. Relax. I'm not gonna bite you." She grinned. "Not unless you want me to."

"Look, I don't want to seem unfriendly, but—"

"Hey, it's okay," she said, removing her arm. "That's some kinda rifle you got there. You with those troops up in Cheyenne?"

"Yeah," he said, then cursed himself for answering. He wished she would stop asking questions.

"Must be really interesting."

He exhaled heavily. "You can say that again."

Her leg moved up against him. "Jesus, you're trembling!

Hey..." She moved closer to him and lowered her voice. "Are you in some kind of trouble?"

"Look, Stormy, I—"

"Cause if you are, it's okay," she said quickly. "I'm not gonna say anything. What'd you do, cut out? Go over the wall or whatever they call it?"

"They call it desertion," Tracy said miserably.

"It's okay. I'm not gonna turn you in or anything. I figure you must've had a reason."

"Yeah. And it's a real doozy."

"Look, you don't have to tell me what it is," she said, dropping her B-girl manner. "I know what it's like to be in trouble, believe me. I've been there."

The waitress finally brought their drinks and stated the charge.

"Look..." said Stormy, "if things are tight, don't worry about it. I can take care of it."

"No, that's all right, thanks. I've got some money. I hocked some of my equipment. But I really appreciate the offer. It was very nice of you."

"Don't mention it. Like I said, I've been there. It's the worst feeling in the world, to be in trouble and not have anyone to turn to. I finally got myself a halfway decent gig, but before I came up with this... well, you probably don't want to know."

He smiled at her. "Thanks."

"For what?"

"For understanding. You're right. About it being the worst feeling in the world, I mean. It's—" He stopped abruptly, looking toward the door with alarm. Two Strike Force officers had entered, and he could see them speaking with the bouncer who'd tried to keep him from bringing in his weapons. "Christ," he said. Linda Tellerman must have turned him in.

Stormy sized up the situation in an instant. "Quick, come with me."

He grabbed his rifle and slid out of the booth, ducking around the corner of the stairway leading down to the runway, following her back toward the restrooms. She led him back to the dancers' dressing room and through the door.

"Wait a minute," he said. "The back door's—"

"If they're looking for you, they might have it covered," she said.

She pulled him into the shabby little dressing room. There were makeup tables piled high with cosmetics dumped out of purses, mirrors, several chairs, a ratty old couch, a wash basin, a carpet heavily scarred with cigarette burns, a stand-up metal clothes rack, some banged-up lockers and not much else. There were two girls in there getting changed. One of them, a brunette, was in jeans and boots, in the act of taking off her bra; the other, a redhead, had on only a blue terry bathrobe and spike heels. She was applying her makeup before one of the mirrors. Both girls looked up as they entered.

"Hey, what the hell . . . ?"

"This is Tracy and he's a friend of mine," said Stormy. "There's some cops out front, lookin' for him. Help me out, okay? We've gotta hide him."

"Come on over here, honey," said the redhead sitting before the mirror. She slid her chair out from the table. "Get under here."

"What?" he said.

"Under the table. Hurry up."

"But they'll see me under there—"

"Don't you worry, hon. They won't be lookin' there, believe me. Sherry, strip down."

He got down on his knees and crawled in under the makeup table, cradling his short battle rifle in his arms, with the safety off, and scrunching himself up in the narrow space between the drawers. Sherry, the brunette, removed her boots, skinned off her jeans and pulled down her panties, then slipped on a pair of spike-heeled black leather boots. The redhead pulled up close to the table, her legs spread wide, on either side of Tracy. His face was perhaps two inches from her vagina. It was shaved, and it had a sexy, musky scent.

"Enjoy the view," she said with a chuckle.

A moment later, the door burst open and the two Strike Force officers entered with their weapons drawn.

"Hey!" said Sherry, the brunette, putting her hands on her hips and striking a pouty pose. "What's the big idea?"

"We're looking for somebody," said one of the Strike Force

cops. But the only place that both of them were looking was directly at Sherry.

"This is our private dressing room," said the redhead, turning slightly, but keeping her chair pulled in close to the table. Her robe completely hid him from view. "Do your looking out front, like everybody else." She went back to applying her eyeliner.

"We're looking for a soldier," said the other cop, his eyes still on Sherry, who smiled at him.

"Well, do we look like soldiers to you?" she said.

"I was sitting out front with a soldier just a few minutes ago," said Stormy, putting a long and attractive leg up on the couch and bending over to adjust one of the black studded straps around her boot, giving them a clear view of her breasts.

"Where... where'd he go?" asked the cop, clearing his throat slightly.

"Said he hadda go back to the john," she said, "but he never did come back. Musta gone out the back way. Stiffed me on my tip, too, the lousy cheapskate."

"He must've seen us come in," said the other cop. "Let's go. We might still catch him."

They left in a hurry.

Tracy heaved a deep sigh of relief.

The redhead shifted back in her chair and looked down at him between her legs. "You just stay under there a little while longer and keep quiet. They might be back."

"I'll go see if they've left," said Stormy, going out the door.

"Just relax and take it easy, hon," the redhead said to Tracy. "It's gonna be all right."

"Thanks," said Tracy. "I really appreciate this."

"Yeah? Prove it," she said softly.

She reached down between her legs and cupped her hand around the back of his head, pulling his face into her crotch.

"Say, 'Thank you, Debbie'," she murmured, pressing him in close.

He mumbled something unintelligible into her vagina and then proceeded to show his gratitude, as directed. Debbie leaned back in the chair, closed her eyes and moaned softly.

"God, Debbie, you're such a nympho," said Sherry, slipping into her costume.

"Mmmmmmm..."

Sherry finished suiting up and went out the door. A short while later, Stormy came back in.

"It's all right, they're gone," she said. "You can come out now."

"Oh, no, no, not yet," said Debbie, arching her back in the chair. "Oh, yes... yes... *yes!*"

"Jesus Christ," said Stormy.

Debbie gasped and shuddered violently. Then, a moment later, she sank back against the chair, her head back and her eyes shut.

"Oooooh... that was *so* nice...."

"Anytime you're ready," Stormy said wryly.

Tracy crawled out sheepishly from underneath the makeup table, wiping his mouth on his sleeve.

"See you guys had a chance to get acquainted," Stormy said dryly.

Tracy blushed. "I... uh..."

"I like your friend," said Debbie, lighting up a cigarette. She smiled. "Bring him back anytime."

"Not unless he's had his shots," said Stormy.

"Meow," said Debbie.

"You got a place to stay?" asked Stormy.

Tracy was still flushed with embarrassment. "No... I..."

"Here, take this," said Stormy, writing out her address on a slip of paper. "It's my apartment. Think you can find it all right?"

"I... no, listen, I couldn't—"

"Just shut up and take it," she said, pressing the slip of paper and a key into his hand. "Here's my spare key. There's some beer in the fridge. I'll be off at twelve."

"No, listen, I can't possibly—"

"If he wants, he can stay at my place," Debbie said slyly.

"Just take it and go," said Stormy, "before those guys come back. We can talk about it when I get home. You're not allergic to cats, are you?"

"No, I like cats."

"Good. I've got four of them, but they're all very nice. They won't bite or scratch or anything."

"Why are you doing this?"

"I told you, I know what it's like to be in trouble. Now go on. Get out of here."

# 7

Steele listened intently while Higgins outlined the situation, then he exhaled heavily. "Jesus Christ. Is there any chance he's bluffing? You think he'd really launch the missiles?"

"The Zach Cord I knew never bluffed," said Higgins grimly. "He might've lost his mind, but I doubt he's lost his nerve."

"Does he actually have the capability to do it?"

"The NSC seems to think he does. He's got everything out there that he needs, all the supplies and plenty of spare parts to get what's left of the network operational, plus the people with the expertise to help him do it."

Steele shook his head. "God damn. Has he issued his ultimatum yet?"

"He called the President a short while ago and presented his demands," said Higgins. "His timing was perfect. He waited about an hour or so after he spoke to me. Just enough time for the President to get the NSC together in an emergency meeting. They were all there when Cord called. He's given us two options. Either we submit to him and execute an orderly transition of authority, or he goes public with the announcement that New York will be ground zero."

"Good God. That'll throw the whole city into a panic."

"That's what he's counting on," said Higgins, nodding. "He doesn't intend to use the missiles except as an absolute last resort. If Congress refuses to capitulate, he'll go on the air with his threat of nuclear blackmail and hope that a civil insurrection will result in the government being overthrown. And they'll do it, too. We'll have the whole population of this city storming the Federal Building. The entire Congress is liable to get lynched." Higgins compressed his lips into a tight grimace. "We've got seventy-two hours. That's how long Cord's given us before he goes on the air with his ultimatum."

"That's if Linda Tellerman doesn't beat him to the punch," said Steele.

"Don't worry, she won't. She won't be going on the air with anything. I had her placed under arrest earlier tonight. She's being held right here in the Federal Building."

"You *arrested* her?" said Steele. "On what charge?"

"Conspiracy to violate the National Security Act. She's being held without bail."

"Can you make it stick?"

"I'm not interested in making the charge stick," said Higgins. "I only want to keep her damn mouth shut until we can figure out what the hell to do. The network's lawyers are all having coronaries, but I've got the President's personnal authority behind me. Miss Tellerman's not going anywhere."

"Did she tell anyone else about this?"

"What, and take the chance of losing her exclusive?" Higgins said wryly.

"Yeah, that would be just like her. How did the media react to her arrest?"

"They ran with it as their lead on the eleven o'clock news," said Higgins. "I've had reporters trying to get through to me all night, but we designated a spokesman to field all their questions with 'no statement at this time' and hold them off with a promise of a press conference tomorrow morning."

"What are you going to tell them?"

"As little as possible. Fortunately, it's not my headache.

State's going to handle it. I've got enough to worry about as it is."

"What about this sergeant, Tracy? Any further word from him?"

"Not yet," said Higgins. "Tellerman wouldn't say where he was, so we shot her up with Pentothal and asked her once again. His last location was some bar in Denver called the Crazy Horse Club, but he told her that if he didn't hear from her within an hour, he wasn't going to stick around. I called the club, but he'd already taken off. The police came by, looking for him. Apparently, they spotted the truck he stole outside the club. Cord sent word to the Denver Strike Force that Tracy was an unstable individual who'd gone off the deep end and went AWOL while he was on guard duty with a full battle kit. Knowing that, the Denver cops will probably shoot first and ask questions later."

"Can you back them off and give the kid some room?"

Higgins shook his head. "I'm afraid not. Cord sent a chopper out to intercept him and Tracy shot it down with a rocket. Police found the wreckage on I-25, near Loveland. There weren't any survivors. So now, in addition to desertion, Tracy's also wanted for murder. If he's smart, he's found someplace to hole up and stay low. If he tries to get in touch with Tellerman again, he'll find out she's been arrested, and he may try to get in touch with me. If he does, I'll try to bring him in. Otherwise, there's really nothing I can do for him. And I can't spare any time worrying about him now."

"I don't suppose there's any way to evacuate the city?"

"Even if we could, Cord could just as easily target Chicago or Boston or any other well-populated city," Higgins said. "We don't even know how many birds he's got out there."

"Looks like he's got you over a barrel. Three days. That's not a lot of time. What the hell can you do in three days?"

"There's only one thing we *can* do," Higgins said. "Assault the base. And that's where you come in."

"You want me to assault an *army* base? You've gotta be kidding. I may be supercop, but I'm not *that* good. What about the military?"

"With the exception of some local troops, none of the other units are responding."

Steele frowned. "What do you mean, they're not responding?"

"I mean we've got a damn mutiny on our hands," said Higgins. "All of a sudden, all our units are 'engaged in hostilities' out in the field. Or there's been some kind of viral outbreak or communications have mysteriously broken down. Cord must've gotten through to all the area commanders. They're sitting on their hands, waiting to see if he can pull it off. Even the Joint Chiefs are recommending that we go along with Cord."

"Christ," said Steele. "So what the hell do you expect *me* to do? Take on a whole damn base all by myself?"

"Of course not. That would be suicide. But I'd like you to take charge of the assault. We can use some local troops that have remained loyal, and I'll get you all the ordnance you'll need. I can give you all the agents and security personnel I've got at my disposal, and we can mobilize the Strike Force and the police department—"

"And leave the city unprotected? The gangs would have a goddamn field day," said Steele. "Besides, word would get out in a flash and you'd have the entire city in a panic."

"I don't see what other choice we've got. Do you?"

"No, not really," said Steele. "Hell, even if we could assault the base, what would prevent Cord from launching the missiles the moment we tried it?"

"Maybe nothing. But according to Linda Tellerman, Tracy told her that the missiles weren't fully operational yet. Cord might still be several days away from having them ready to launch. That could be the reason for the seventy-two hour deadline. Tracy forced him to move up his schedule. If we can hit them fast enough and hard enough—"

"You'd still be taking one hell of a chance," said Steele.

"I don't see any alternative. Our only chance is to hit the base and take out Cord before he can launch the birds. Without him, the whole thing will probably fall apart. It's either that or surrender the government to him."

"What happens if you agree to capitulate?" asked Steele. "It could buy us some time. You could send some representatives out to negotiate with Cord, and when the assault came down, they could deny that the government had anything to do with it."

"He'd never buy it."

"He might. Especially if he knows the military is playing a waiting game to see if he can pull it off. If we go in with choppers and heavy armor, he'll know that the government's behind it, but what if the base was hit by outlaw raiders?"

"Raiders?" said Higgins, frowning.

"It's a long shot," said Steele, "but if he buys it, it just might keep him from launching the missiles. Cord knows there are several large, well-organized outlaw gangs in his part of the country, raiders who've hit federal arsenals and equipped themselves with ordnance. His troops have probably gone up against some of them. We could get a bunch of civilian vehicles together: 4 X 4s, trucks, jeeps, motorcycles, maybe a few 'stolen' military dueces. Get a few C-17s out of Newark, bring 'em in to La Guardia, load up and fly in as low as possible to stay off radar. Take off at night and follow a flight path plotted to keep us well away from any military units out in the field, so they can't spot us and send word ahead to Cord. We could set up an LZ within striking distance of the base and launch a mobile ground assault, so it'll look like a large band of raiders trying to hit the base for ordnance and supplies."

"I doubt he'd fall for that," said Higgins. "Cord isn't stupid."

"I'm not assuming he is," said Steele, "which is why I'm thinking of using the real thing. We'll use all the soldiers and agents you can get, plus retired Strike Force personnel and cops, private security, anyone we can drum up in a hurry, but I'm also talking about using real outlaws. Long hair, beards, colors, the works. There'll be no mistaking them for regular troops. We can salt the other people in among them."

"You can't be serious!"

"Why not? Ice still has a lot of gang people who are loyal to him out in no-man's-land. And The Brood will do just about anything if the money's right. Hell, they're so hardcore crazy, they're liable to get off on something like this."

"That's insane," said Higgins. "You're talking about sending a bunch of untrained hoodlums and psychotics against some of the most finely disciplined troops in the entire world. That would be like sending the Hells Angels out to take on the Israeli Army!"

"You got any other suggestions?"

Higgins sighed and ran his hand through his hair. He looked exhausted. "No, damn it, I don't. You think you can actually convince a bunch of outlaws to throw in with us?"

"I can try. But it'll take some pretty strong incentives."

"Yeah, I figured that. But I don't know how much we can scare up in a hurry. We can offer them ordnance, of course. What about drugs? You think they'd take a payoff in drugs?"

"You've got drugs?"

Higgins grimaced. "The kind of budget we've had to work with, we had to make ends meet somehow. Yeah, we've got drugs."

"Some outfit I'm working for," said Steele wryly. "I spend half my life trying to put the pushers out of business and here you are, supplying them." He shook his head with disbelief. "You're a real piece of work, Higgins."

"Save me the sermon, okay? Will they take drugs in payment or won't they?"

"What the hell do *you* think? The way things are these days, the damn drugs are more stable than the currency."

"Okay, then. Get hold of Ice. I'll see what I can come up with. You got any contacts with The Brood?"

"Not really, but I've crossed paths with a few of them before. I'll take a chopper out to Montauk and see if I can swing a deal with them."

Higgins nodded. "Okay, get on it. We need to move fast. We've only got three days. Christ. Cord's got Rangers, Delta Force and Cobras and we're gonna send out a bunch of retired cops, scooter trash and junkies to take them on. What a joke. They'll all get cut to ribbons."

"Maybe," Steele said.

"*Maybe*? What're you, kidding me?"

"They've had to learn how to survive out there in no-man's-land, where every day's a goddamn war," said Steele. "They may not be trained and disciplined troops, but I wouldn't write them off so quickly."

"Yeah, well, playing cowboys and indians with the cops is

one thing," Higgins said. "We're talking about taking on the Cobra Force, for Christ's sake. Those guys are a fucking nightmare. I oughta know. I helped Cord train them."

"They don't need to beat the Cobra Force," said Steele. "Just keep them busy long enough for me to get inside the base and find Cord."

Higgins thought it over for a moment, then nodded. "All right. What the hell, it's worth a shot. And we haven't got a lot of options. It's your operation. You call it. What do you want me to do?"

"Start commandeering those vehicles and arranging transport," Steele said. "And get your resources together. Cash, weapons, dope, whatever the hell you can get your hands on in a hurry. And stand by with choppers to deliver the goods. I won't be in much position to negotiate. We don't have time to haggle with the warlords. Whatever the gangs want, we'll have to meet their price. Get as many trained personnel together as you can and tell them to dress casual. You know what I mean. No washing, no shaving. The rattier they look, the better. For the sake of security, you'd better not tell them any more than they need to know, but make sure they understand just how bad the odds are. I only want volunteers. We'll also need a staging area for the operation. A couple of large warehouses ought to do. Pick out something in no-man's-land to attract the least amount of attention. Take care of that first, so I can tell our people where to report."

"Okay, I'll get on it right away."

"I'll stop by my place, pick up my gear, coordinate with Ice, then head straight out to Montauk. Have Doctor Stone standing by on the broadcast link. I'll want to keep in touch."

"Right. Good luck."

"Yeah, you too. Who knows, if we can pull this off, they might even give you back your budget."

Higgins snorted. "If we pull this off, they'll probably just give me a commendation and retire me with a pension. Hell, I'd just as soon catch it from a bullet in Wyoming."

"You mean you intend to come along?" said Steele, surprised.

"Well, I'm sure as hell not going to sit around here and wait for Cord to drop a Peacekeeper in my lap," said Higgins.

"Besides, I've been behind this goddamn desk too long. It's past time I got my hands dirty again."

Steele smiled. "Okay, then. Let's *do* it."

Stormy's place was on the top floor of a dilapidated, three-story Victorian on Elizabeth Street. Actually, it was four floors up, since it was located in the attic. At some point in the distant past, the house had been divided into small apartments. A narrow stairway had been added, leading up to a small, finished loft in the attic. The interior of the roof had been insulated and covered with drywall, so that the walls were only about four feet high along the sides before they met the angles of the roof. The door opened into a small living room, which led into a tiny kitchenette and then a bathroom, located squarely in the middle of the loft. It was necessary to go through the bathroom door, walk through the narrow space between the plastic-curtained bathtub/shower and the sink and toilet, then through another door to get into the bedroom at the rear of the apartment.

Stormy's "bed" consisted of an old mattress lying on the floor, with a couple of plastic milk crates placed on either side of it for nightstands. There were no carpets, except for a small, braided, oval throw rug in the front room. A worn and stained old futon served as a couch in the living room, and there was an old armchair badly in need of reupholstering, with the legs either sawn or broken off. There was an old coffee table, with the finish almost completely worn off; some bookshelves made up of boards placed across stacks of old bricks; a desk that consisted of an old hollow-core door placed across two scratched and dented filing cabinets, a chair, a couple of small desk lamps and several candles stuck in bottles or melted into place on old, chipped plates. She had about a dozen or so clay pots with ivy growing in them to provide a touch of greenery, and most of her books were ancient, well-worn paperbacks, mostly fantasy and science fiction with a sprinkling of mysteries.

There were a number of old posters thumbtacked to the sloping walls—one of a voluptuous, dark-haired woman dressed in some kind of animal-skin bikini and furry boots, standing in a dramatic pose with her bare legs spread; another depicted a pretty, androgynous-looking young black man with his hair in wavy little ringlets. He was in the act of singing, holding a microphone, his mouth open and his head thrown back. There was another print of a unicorn with its head in the lap of a young maiden in a long, diaphanous white gown and several pen and ink sketches that either Stormy or one of her friends had done, drawings of elves, wizards and topless female centaurs. They were rather good. Tracy noticed that each of them was signed with the initials "K.C." in a circle.

The apartment smelled decidedly of cats and there was a litter box in the bathroom that needed emptying. Three cats came mewling up to greet him, a short-haired tabby, a caramel-colored, Persian mix and a skinny Siamese. The fourth, a big fat black cat with white whiskers, a white blaze on his nose and one white paw, regarded him with regal indifference from atop the desk. There was no phone.

Stormy was apparently not very big on housekeeping. Clothes were wadded up and piled here and there, there were empty bottles on the coffee table and the desk, the sink was full of dishes and the ash trays were full of cigarette butts. Tracy put down his rifle and went over to look inside the refrigerator. It held a dozen cans of Coors beer from the brewery in nearby Golden, a carton of milk, an opened can of cat food, a half-empty carton of eggs, a thoroughly wilted head of lettuce, a small tub of margarine, half a loaf of whole wheat bread, a large bag of marijuana, some apples and some moldy cheese. There were more cosmetics in the bathroom than there was food in the refrigerator.

What the hell, thought Tracy. He took out a can of beer, popped it open and, for lack of anything better to do, started cleaning up. She took a complete stranger into her home, such as it was, he figured the least he could do was wash the dishes and empty out the ashtrays. But nervous energy kept him going, and four beers later, he'd cleaned up the whole apartment. It wasn't quite up to the standards of a base inspection, but it was probably the cleanest it had ever been. Then exhaustion finally claimed him and he sank down on the futon with his rifle on the floor beside him, took his pistol out of its holster and put it by his side, pulled off his boots and went to sleep.

He was awakened several hours later by the sound of her key in the door. Two of the cats were curled up beside him.

She came in, wearing tight, faded jeans, running shoes, a sweatshirt and a leather motorcycle jacket. She was carrying a bag of groceries. She used her back to shut the door.

"You made it! Great. I didn't know if you'd be here, but I figured I'd pick up some food just in case and . . . Holy shit!"

"What is it?" he said, alarmed.

"What the hell did you *do*?"

"Oh. I was feeling a little wired, so I thought I'd just clean up a bit. I hope you don't mind."

"*Mind?* Are you kidding? Jesus, look at this place! It's spotless! You didn't have to go to all this trouble!"

He shrugged. "You went to a lot of trouble for me. I don't know if I put everything away the way you like it, I sorta had to guess."

"Wow. You even emptied the litter box. Jeez, you must think I'm a real slob."

"No, I think you're a very nice person for helping me the way you did. You don't even know anything about me. You took a pretty big chance. I could've been some sort of freak or something."

She put the bag of groceries down on the kitchen table. "I didn't think there was much chance of that. I can usually spot the bad ones. Believe me, I've had lots of experience. You just seemed like you were a nice guy who got himself in trouble. But hey, you didn't have to do all this."

"It's no big deal. It helped me work off some nervous energy and get some sleep. I was dead on my feet. I really appreciate what you've done, Stormy. Thanks."

"Karen."

"What?"

"Karen. Stormy's just the name I dance under. My real name's Karen Carter. My friends call me K.C."

"You did those drawings?"

"Huh?"

"The sketches on the walls. I was looking at them. They're really very good."

"Thank you." She kicked off her shoes and sat down. "Somebody called the club and asked for you."

"A woman?"

"No, some guy. You know anyone named Higgins?"

Higgins?" Tracy frowned. "No."

"Well, he seemed to know you."

"Wait a minute," Tracy said. He took a folded piece of paper out of his breast pocket. He unfolded it and looked at it. "Yeah, I know who he is. He's CIA."

"CIA?" she said. "You've got the *CIA* after you? Jesus, what did you *do*?"

"I tried to stop a military coup."

"A what?"

"A military coup. That's when the army takes over control of the government."

"You're kidding."

"Believe me, I wish I was. Look, you took a big chance helping me the way you did, so I might as well tell you the whole story. You deserve to know what you've gotten yourself into."

She lit up a cigarette. She offered him the pack, he took one and she lit it for him.

"I was part of the unit sent up to Warren Air Force Base out in Cheyenne. Our job was supposed to be to deactivate the missile network out there."

"There's still missiles up there?" she said. "I thought they were all launched during the war."

"Not all of them. The virus killed some of the launch crews before they could complete their launch procedures. So there are still missiles up there, standing in their silos. We were supposed to crack open the silos and LCFs—that's the Launch Control Facilities—take an inventory and dismantle the remaining missiles. General Cord was placed in command of the operation since he's the area commander of the entire Northwest Sector, and some government scientists were sent out from back east to supervise the whole thing. Only Cord hasn't dismantled any of the missiles. He never intended to. Instead, he took the scientists prisoner and forced them to show him how to bring the missiles back on line. Replace the burned-out computer components, get the missiles operational again and retarget them."

"What for?"

"He's going to use them to blackmail the government into

giving him control. Either they turn the government over to him, or he drops a nuke on New York City."

"My God! Are you *serious*?"

"Deadly serious. I was on one of the details in charge of opening up the silos and the LCFs, and I knew from the start something was screwy. Every time we opened up a silo or an LCF, a maintenance crew went down there and started checking out the systems and replacing parts. The official story was that they needed to get all the equipment operational again so they could check out the status of the missiles, but it just didn't ring true somehow. I couldn't see why they needed to get them back on line just to dismantle the network. Why not just remove the warheads and take the damn things apart? And on top of that, Cord had several elite combat units flown in, supposedly to provide additional security. But he already had the Cobra Force there, in addition to the regular troops. What the hell did he need Rangers and Delta Force for? It just didn't make sense. It's like he was expecting a war or something.

"And then, last night, while I was getting ready to go on guard duty, I ran into one of the scientists. A man named Doctor Franks. They were keeping them all under guard in one of the officers' mansions, again supposedly to provide them with security, but Franks told me what was really going on. And everything clicked right in. I knew he was telling me the truth. He'd escaped and he was trying to get off base to warn the authorities. But the Cobras caught up to him and took him back. There wasn't anything that I could do. If I had tried to stop them, they would have shot me. One of them almost did. They were suspicious, but I managed to convince them that Franks hadn't had a chance to tell me anything. And then, first chance I got, I went over the wall. I stole a truck in Cheyenne. I figured if I could make Denver before they found out I was gone, I could lose myself in the city and warn them."

"And did you?" she said. "Warn them, I mean."

"I tried. I got through to Linda Tellerman, the network newscaster. You know, the one who did those stories on the cyborg? I was pretty sure I had convinced her, but then when the cops showed up at the club, I thought she'd given me away. But maybe she didn't. I tried to get back to my truck . . . well, the truck I stole . . . and the cops were watching it, so maybe they just spotted it outside the club. And they might've got a report from that pawnshop where I hocked some of my gear. But Linda was supposed to call me back at the club and she never did. Instead, this guy Higgins calls. I don't know what that means. She said he was the one she contacted with the information I gave her and she gave me his number, but she also said she didn't tell him where I was. And the only way he could've known that was if she told him. So I don't know what the hell to think now."

"Wow," said K.C. "So the cops were after you because you deserted and you stole a truck. Hell, that's not so bad. Sounds to me like you had one hell of a good reason. And it's not as if you killed anybody or anything like that."

Tracy looked at her and compressed his lips tightly. "Only I did. At least two people, maybe more. I don't know."

"You don't *know*?"

"They sent a chopper out to intercept me on the way to Denver. It caught up to me outside Loveland. I had to shoot it down. I don't know how many people were aboard. At least two. Maybe more."

"You shot down an *army helicopter*?" she said with disbelief. She glanced at his battle rifle. "With *that*?"

"No, with my rocket launcher. I sold it to a pawnshop to get some money. I didn't have any on me when I left. Actually, to be perfectly honest, what I did was rob the pawnshop. The guy figured I was AWOL and he tried to rook me on the deal, so I held him up and cleaned out his cash register. About six hundred dollars. But I left the rocket launcher, the backpack computer and my battle helmet. He came out way ahead on the deal, but that still doesn't change the fact that I held him up at gunpoint. So I'm not only a deserter, I'm also a car thief, an armed robber and a murderer. And by coming here, I'm afraid I've made you an accessory."

"What would've happened if you hadn't shot down that helicopter?"

"They would've killed me, or arrested me and taken me back, which would've amounted to the same thing, I guess. I would've been court-martialed and shot, probably."

"So it was self-defense, then."

Tracy made a sound halfway between a snort and a laugh.

"Somehow, I don't think the police would see it that way."

"Well, I don't give a shit how the police would see it, that's how it looks to me. You stole the car because you had to, and you could've just held up the pawnshop without leaving your stuff there. Like you said, it's not like the guy lost out on the deal. That stuff must be worth a hell of lot more than a lousy six hundred bucks."

"But it wasn't mine to sell," he said.

"Who cares? Look, what are you beating yourself over the head for? From what you told me, it sounds to me like you're a hero, not a criminal, for Christ's sake!"

Tracy grimaced. "Somehow, I'm not feeling very heroic at the moment. What I feel is scared."

"Well, believe me, I know what that feels like," she said. "But you should be pretty safe here. Nobody knows you're here except Debbie and Sherry, and they won't say anything. They're friends of mine and cops aren't exactly their favorite people."

"Yeah, maybe not, but what if there's a reward out? I mean, I don't want to say anything against your friends, but people can be tempted, you know?"

"Depends on who's doing the tempting," she said. "Sherry's boyfriend was shot down by the cops, and Debbie served some time for dealing. Believe me, even if there was a reward, they wouldn't turn you in. Snitch is a dirty word in this part of town. Besides, I think Debbie kinda likes you."

Tracy blushed. "Yeah, well . . . about what happened with Debbie . . . I . . . Hell, I don't really know what to say."

"So you went down on her. What's wrong with that? Knowing her, she probably got turned on with the cops questioning her about you and you right there between her legs." She giggled. "Jesus, you're actually blushing! You're so damn straight, I can't believe it!"

Tracy blushed again and looked away. "I feel like a damn idiot."

"Come on. You're just a nice guy who got in way over his head." She giggled at her unintentional pun. "In more ways than one."

"Look, I'm grateful for everything you've done," said Tracy, "but maybe I should just get out of here. I've already involved you too much. I don't want to see you get in trouble on my account."

"Are you kidding? Some whacked-out general is getting ready to drop a bomb on New York City and kill God knows how many people, and you're worried about one exotic dancer? Come on, get serious. Besides, where the hell would you go?"

"I've got some money—"

"Yeah, and in this neighborhood, how long do you think you'll keep it?"

"I'm not exactly unprotected, you know." He patted his battle rifle. "And I've got my pistol, my knife, and plenty of ammunition."

"Sure. And you'll check into some sleazy strip motel, and the manager will make a call, let the creeps in with his passkey and they'll plug you while you're sleeping. Or some gang sniper will take you out. Walking around with that thing is a sure invitation to get yourself trashed."

"I may seem a bit naive to you," said Tracy defensively, "but I've been in combat, you know. I can take care of myself."

"Honey, being in combat's one thing, but you're on the Denver Strip now. And no offense, but you're a real babe in the woods. Besides, you think you can lay all that stuff on me and just *leave*? Forget about it! We've got to *do* something!"

"Look, don't think I'm ungrateful, but I can't think what I can accomplish just by staying here."

"You can stay alive, for one thing. The cops are looking for you, but they're not looking for me. And this is *my* turf. I know it like the back of my hand. You can do a lot more with me than without me. So just knock off this 'I-don't-want-to-get-you-into-trouble' routine. I've been in trouble all my life. Now the first thing we've gotta do is find out what the story is with this news reporter you've been in touch with. And then we'll find out what the deal is with this Higgins guy. After that, I'll make a couple of calls. I might know some people who can help you. But first we gotta get some food into you. You look like you're about to pass out."

Tracy grimaced. "I already did."

"Well, you cleaned up the place, the least I can do is make you dinner. You like chili?"

"I love it."

"Hot?"

"The hotter, the better."

"Hey, a man after my own heart. I'll make us some dinner, but first, what say we crack open a couple of brews and break out the bong to help work up our appetites?"

She got up and went over to the fridge. She took out the bag of grass.

"That's marijuana, isn't it?" said Tracy.

She stared at him. "You're putting me on."

"Yeah, well . . . that's what I figured it was."

"Oh, wow. You mean to tell me you've *never* gotten high?"

"Well, I've been drunk a few times."

She rolled her eyes. "My God. I've got a virgin on my hands." She went over to her desk and picked up a plastic bong pipe, then came over to sit on the futon beside him. "Don't worry, you're not gonna hallucinate or anything. But you might feel a little silly. It affects some people that way."

He watched as she prepared the pipe and lit it. She placed her mouth over the bong and inhaled deeply, held it, then let it out in a heavy exhalation.

"Okay, now just do like I did," she said, passing him the pipe.

He copied her, but he was unprepared for the harshness of the smoke. He started coughing.

She chuckled. "It's okay, you'll get used to it. It'll help you relax. After what you've been through, you need to mellow out a little."

They passed the bong back and forth a few times, then she looked at him and smiled. "Feeling it yet?"

"A little."

"Open your mouth."

"What?"

"Open your mouth. I'm going to supercharge you."

He opened his mouth. She took a deep drag on the bong, then, holding it, she leaned over, put her arm around him, and placing her mouth up against his, she exhaled into him. He felt her warm breath and the hot smoke fill up his lungs.

"I'm feeling a little lightheaded," he said.

"That's the whole idea." She put down the pipe. "Don't want to overdo it the first time."

He blinked. "Whew."

She smiled. "Come here."

She cupped her hands around his face and kissed him very lightly, then ran her tongue over his lips. She moved against him, her tongue slipping into his mouth. He brought his hand up to caress her breast. She took his wrist and he hesitated. He started to apologize, but she smiled and slipped his hand inside her sweatshirt. She wasn't wearing a bra. She kissed him again as he fondled her.

She reached down between his legs. "You have done *this* before, haven't you?"

"Uh, yeah, once or twice."

"Mmmmm," she said, undoing his trousers. She lowered her head to his lap.

"Oh, Jesus . . ." he said, leaning back and shutting his eyes.

A few moments later, she stopped, got up and took off her sweatshirt, then peeled off her jeans. She wasn't wearing any panties and she was a natural blond.

"God," he said, his eyes glazed. "You're so beautiful. . . ."

She grinned. "And you're *so* stoned. . . ."

She pushed him back down onto the futon.

The X-wing came in low over the town of Montauk, out on the southeastern tip of Long Island. They had flown at close to the speed of sound over long stretches of deserted southern Long Island countryside, broken up here and there by tiny settlements. They followed the old Sunrise Expressway, and as they approached the Hamptons, near where the eastern end of Long Island split into two finlike projections separated by the Great Peconic Bay, they dropped their airspeed down below 200 mph. As the graphite fiber X-wings switched from fixed wing to rotary blade mode, the craft reverted from a jet back to a helicopter once again. They passed over the sprawling agro-communes operated by The Brood, farm settlements that did not supply the city, but fed the villages governed by The Brood Enclave and sold their produce to the other outlaw enclaves on the island and to freebooters plying the Atlantic Coast.

The towns of Westhampton, Hampton Bays, Southhampton,

Bridgehampton and East Hampton, collectively referred to as "The Hamptons," had at one time been the summer playground of the city's wealthy celebrities and literati, where would-be F. Scott Fitzgeralds rubbed elbows with movie stars and rock musicians. Now, they were once more sleepy little seacoast towns and fishing villages, home to those survivors of the Bio War who had gone to The Brood to seek protection from the scavengers and raiders who found shelter in the island's many ghost towns.

Steele had requested a data download on The Brood before he left and Dr. Stone had gotten it together for him while he was meeting Ice. As they flew out toward Montauk in the X-wing, Jennifer contacted him through the broadcast link and fed the information to him. "The brotherhood," as they sometimes referred to themselves, was originally formed sometime after the Bio War, when the surviving members of several large outlaw motorcycle clubs from the tri-state area banded together to form The Brood. Their colors were black leather vests emblazoned with a grinning death's head with long blonde hair and an Uncle Sam top hat worn at a rakish angle. Above it was a white rocker with "Brood" embroidered on it in red letters, below it, a similar rocker bearing the words "Long Island." On either side of the skull were two smaller patches, one with the letter "M," the other with the letter "C." On closer inspection, one could see small nuclear mushroom clouds in the death head's eye sockets.

The term "outlaw motorcycle club" apparently did not originally refer to outlaws in the commonly accepted definition of the term. In the days after World War II, a number of loosely organized biker clubs sprang up, perhaps the most famous originating with a group of freewheeling veterans who adopted the name of their former combat squadron—the Hells Angels. The American Motorcycle Association, the body that sanctioned racing events that were, up to that time, the chief focus of organized biker activity, did not approve of these raucous, hard-drinking, brawling hellraisers who attended their functions and consequently branded them as "outlaws"—meaning that they had no respect for that organization's bylaws—and, conscious of its public image, referred to them as only "one percent" of the motorcycling enthusiast population. Whereupon the clubs proudly started to refer to themselves as "outlaws" and "one percenters."

According to the file, if their lifestyle and image in later years could be pinned down to one event, it would have been the famous "raid" on the small town of Hollister, Texas, an incident that was greatly exaggerated in the press and exaggerated even further in a Hollywood film based on that event, *The Wild One*, starring Marlon Brando. Real bikers considered Lee Marvin to be the true star of that film for his authentic portrayal of a boozing, two-fisted one percenter, but it was Brando, with his sultry good looks and jaunty cap, who received all the attention in his star-making role as the leather-jacketed leader of the fictional Black Rebels Motorcycle Club. And he didn't even ride a Harley, but a Triumph, which real one percenters conceded was a motorcycle, but just barely. That film, more than anything else, firmly established the image of the "outlaw motorcycle gang" in the public's mind. Lock the doors, call the state police and hide your daughters, here come the "outlaw bikers" to take over your town. People expected the worst from one percenters after that and, perversely, the one percenters gave it to them.

In The Brood's case, they had literally taken over not one, but several towns. And the beleaguered citizens were only too glad to have them do so. Few of the current members of the "brotherhood" had even heard of Marlon Brando, much less *The Wild One*. That had been long before their time. But they had a long tradition on which to draw, and these modern motorcycle outlaws were outlaws in every sense of the term. At least insofar as the government was concerned, since they recognized absolutely no authority outside their own. It took a lot more than a motorcycle and a leather jacket to be a member of The Brood. In their own way, they were as much of an elite as were the Cobras and the Delta Force. A "prospect" had to prove himself over a period of time. (Never *her*self; The Brood had women, but they weren't an equal opportunity organization. Women could belong, but only as defined by marriage or an intimate relationship. On their colors, they wore small patches identifying them as the "property" of a particular member.) And time spent as a "prospect" could make indentured servitude seem like an attractive lifestyle.

In the years since they had established their enclave, The Brood had brought law and order to their part of the island. *Their* law and *their* order, enforced with Draconian effectiveness. But they had also brought a measure of stability and prosperity to the citizens who resided in their towns and agrocommunes. Life in The Brood Enclave was, in many ways, much safer than life in Midtown, and it was immeasurably preferable to life in Midtown's no-man's-land. There wasn't a raider or a screamer within miles of their turf, and anyone who broke their laws was dealt with quickly, efficiently, and often, permanently. They did business with the freebooters and the mob enclaves to the west, who kept them supplied with precious fuel and various other commodities that they could not produce in their machine shops. They maintained fishing fleets, a power plant, manufacturing facilities and even a small hospital. In short, they were essentially autonomous. They wanted nothing from the government, and since they posed no threat to it and ran no criminal operations in the city, as did the mobs, the government left them alone and asked nothing from them.

Except this time.

The X-wing slowed as it approached the town of Montauk, headquarters of The Brood Enclave. Word of their approach had already reached the headquarters and the pilot, his head totally enclosed inside his VCASS helmet, indicated a spot below them, where a large number of bikes had formed a circle in an open area, defining an LZ. The message was quite clear. Land *here*. Steele glanced at the pilot and nodded.

They set down inside the circle of bikes, and as the rotors slowed, the pilot turned to Steele and asked, "You think this'll take long?"

"I hope not," Steele said. "I haven't got the luxury of time."

"I'll stay with the chopper then. My luck, one of these jokers will know how to fly this thing and they might decide they want an air force."

Steele grinned. "If they decide that, you being here's not going to stop them."

"Maybe not, but it might discourage them a little," said the pilot, patting his machine pistol.

"Just don't get nervous," Steele said. "If they get the idea that you're tense, they might try to push you, so stay cool."

"You got it."

Steele left the chopper, ducking to avoid the rotating blades as they slowed. The graphite fiber blades were rigid and they weren't supposed to flex and droop like standard blades, but he wasn't taking any chances. He still remembered the time an overeager Strike Force trainee of considerably more than average height disembarked fully upright from a chopper on a training exercise. Fortunately, the blades had slowed enough so that his mistake was not a lethal one, but one of the drooping blades beaned him in the back of his battle helmet and he went down like a felled tree. After that, every time he got out of a chopper, he looked like he was crawling through a mine tunnel.

Three of the motorcycles roared up to meet him, a Harley Sport Glide and two ratty Honda Hurricanes, looking like gutted mixmasters with all the plastic aerodynamic bodywork removed. Without the sleek, wraparound bodywork, they were ugly-looking things, wires, cables and oil lines hanging out all over the place. In the old days, one percenters would sooner chug-a-lug spitoons than ride on Japanese machinery, which they referred to contemptuously as "ricegrinders," but in these hard times, good wheels were hard to come by. Consequently, the old Harley-Davidsons, regardless of condition, were symbols of serious status.

The Harley that pulled up to him was stripped down and more closely resembled a two-wheeled tractor, what with its lack of a windshield and front fender, its frame-hugging seat and homemade components to replace worn-out original parts, but its straight pipes gave stentorian testimony to the motor's soundness, and every square inch of the beautiful, bored and stroked V-twin engine had been lovingly cleaned and polished. The large, five-gallon gas tank was painted a deep, midnight blue, with almost photographically perfect Colt Single Action Army revolvers rendered on its sides. Steele recognized the hulking rider. He was known as "Peacemaker," the club's sergeant-at-arms. They had never met before, but Steele had seen him interviewed on a television talk show about the outlaw enclaves on Long Island.

The Harley roared up to him and slid to a stop with its front wheel about an inch from Steele's kneecap. Steele stood his ground and didn't flinch, as he was undoubtedly intended to. The giant biker regarded him steadily for a long moment, taking him in. Steele, in turn, took the biker's measure. He must have weighed close to three hundred pounds, with a huge beer gut and arms like tree trunks, festooned with intricate tattoos. His hair hung well below his shoulders, and his full beard came down to his chest. He looked like a viking. He had heavy rings on all four fingers of each hand, which probably gave his fists the effect of knuckledusters in a fight, and he wore gold earrings in both ears, as well as one in his nose, like a prize bull.

"What happens when you have to blow your nose?" asked Steele, pleasantly.

In reply, the biker made a loud, snorting noise and hocked a huge lunger onto Steele's boot.

Steele glanced down at it, then looked up at the outlaw and smiled. Then he reached down quickly, stuck his fingers through the front wheel's spokes, grabbing it by the rim, and lifted the entire front end one-handed, dumping the startled biker on his ass.

Instantly, an entire battery of guns was pointed at him. Steele paid no attention. As the biker sat on the ground, staring at him in disbelief, Steele carefully lowered the big Harley, steadied it by its handlebar and put down the kickstand. Then he bent over and blew an imaginary speck of dust off the gas tank.

For a moment, there was total silence. Then Peacekeeper started to laugh; a big, booming, raucous "Haw-haw-haw-haw!" that immediately broke the tension.

Back inside the chopper, the pilot rolled his eyes and exhaled heavily.

"Fuckin'-A" the outlaw said. "Only one man coulda done that. You're Donovan Steele, aren'tcha?"

"That's me."

The biker got up and held out his hand. "Peacemaker, sergeant-at-arms."

Steele gave him the biker's handshake.

"Put 'em away, boys," Peacemaker said to the others. "This here's one *baaad* motherfucker."

"Nice scooter," said Steele.

"Yeah, thanks for not droppin' it. If ya had, we would've had to dance. Don't think I would've enjoyed that much." He grinned. "So. What does the Man want with the brotherhood?"

"Not the Man," said Steele. "Me. The Man's behind me, but this was my idea. I need to talk some business with your president, and it happens to be real urgent. Can you call a war council?"

Peacemaker frowned. "A *war council*? You know what that means?"

"Yes, I know. Can we do it right away?"

"Damn. What the hell have you got on your mind?"

"I'll make a deal with you, Steele said. "You set it up within fifteen minutes and I'll get you one of those." He pointed at the gun painted on the Harley's gas tank.

"A Peacemaker? You shittin' me?"

"An authentic Colt .45 Single Action Army, not a replica. I know where I can get one. With genuine ivory grips."

"Fuckin'-A, man, you got a *deal*! Hop aboard!"

Ten minutes later, Steele was sitting in the clubhouse bar, surrounded by ten very serious members of The Brood war council. He laid it out for them, then waited for their reaction.

Snake, the club president, sat with his booted feet up on the table, smoking a cigarette. He was as long and lean as his namesake, cleanshaven, with deeply sunken pink eyes, hollow cheeks, and a long knife scar on his face. He was anywhere from thirty to fifty years old, it was impossible to tell. He was an albino, with long, snow white hair that hung straight down to the middle of his back. With his skin stretched taut across his features, he resembled the death's head on the club colors. He was very soft-spoken, with a cool, no nonsense manner and the most penetrating, direct stare that Steele had ever seen.

"Let me get this straight," he said softly. The room was utterly silent. "This General Cord, he wants to set himself up as military dictator, and if the Man doesn't buckle under, he starts launching nukes?"

"That's right. We've got less than seventy-two hours to meet his terms, so I'm in no position to haggle. Name your terms, I'll meet them. Cash, drugs, ordnance, whatever, half payable up front, half after. Assuming there's an after."

Snake stared at him for a long moment without saying anything. "You want us to take on the Cobra Force, huh?"

"That's right. And I need an answer now. Want me to leave the room while you discuss it?"

"America under martial law?" Another long silence. Then Snake addressed the others without shifting his glance from Steele. "We got anything to discuss, people?"

"Fuck no, man!"

"Do it!"

"Waste the bastards!"

"Yeah, let's *party*!"

"You got your answer, Steele," Snake said.

"Thanks. I owe you guys. What are your terms?"

"We don't want nuthin' from the Man," said Snake. "We take the Man's pay, that means we're workin' for the Man and we don't work for *nobody*."

Steele stared at him with astonishment. "There's going to be heavy losses. You telling me you don't want *anything*?"

"Yeah, I want something," Snake said. "You ride?"

"Yeah, I can ride a bike."

Snake stood up and removed his colors, then tossed them on the table before Steele. "When we go in, wear that."

Steele picked up the leather vest emblazoned with the club colors and Snake's name. "I know what these mean to you people," he said. "Why? I haven't done anything to earn it."

"I appreciate that," Snake said. "The Angels used to have a saying. 'When we do right, no one remembers. When we do wrong, no one forgets.' " He smiled. "You're famous, man. We ride against the Cobra Force with a cyborg flyin' our colors, ain't *no one* gonna forget."

Steele stood up and solemnly put on the colors. "It'll be an honor."

They shook, then Snake turned to the others. "Okay. Spread the word. *We ride!*"

# 8

"Who the hell *is* this?"

"Am I talking to Oliver Higgins?"

"Yeah, I'm Higgins. My secretary said you were calling for Sgt. Tracy."

"That's right. I'm not gonna tell you my real name. You can call me Jane Doe. Look, I know you're after him. If you try to trace this call, it won't help you because I'm calling from a public phone and I'll be long gone before anyone can get here."

"Give me a break, kid," Higgins said. "I don't give a damn what your real name is or where you are and I'm not after Tracy. I don't give a damn where he is, either. I've got more important things to worry about."

"Like a nuke falling on New York, you mean?"

"Yeah, like that. Look, I don't have a lot of time. Tell Tracy that I called the club because I was trying to help him out. Linda Tellerman didn't give him away. I had her arrested and shot up with Pentothal. I didn't want her going on the air with this and starting a panic. And if you're smart, you'll keep your mouth shut about it, too. Tell Tracy that he got the job done. We believe him. I've spoken with Cord myself, and he's already contacted the President with his demands. We've got about forty-eight hours before Cord goes public with the threat. We're on it, okay? Tell Tracy if he wants to come in, to call this number in about an hour and ask for Doctor Stone. If he doesn't trust me, tell him to stay low and sit tight. Whatever happens, he'll know about it by Friday."

"What are you gonna do?" she asked, but Higgins had already hung up. She replaced the receiver on its hook and bit her lower lip, then picked up the receiver once again, dropped in a coin and started to dial a number she never thought she'd call again.

They had been arriving all throughout the day, dribbling into the warehouse individually and in small groups. Several trucks had already gone out to La Guardia, ferrying them out. This would be the last load. There were so few of them. So pathetically few. Gang members, hired thugs, retired Strike Force personnel, retired agents, *retired* gang members, for Christ's sake, private security guards who had once been on the NYPD, active Strike Force personnel who could be spared from duty ... perhaps a couple of hundred all told, if that. And, with few exceptions, they were a pretty sorry-looking lot. Higgins stood by the door alongside Jake Hardesty, captain of the Strike Force. Ice had already gone out with the first load. Outside, in the street, a small SCAT chopper sat waiting to fly them out to La Guardia.

"It's hopeless," Hardesty said grimly. "We haven't got anywhere *near* enough men. They'll all be slaughtered."

"We've still got a unit of volunteers coming out from the base in New Jersey," Higgins said. "And Steele's supposed to be coming out with some people from The Brood Enclave. He sent his pilot back. He's riding out with them."

"Great," said Hardesty wryly. "We're going to try to take on Cord's entire command with a few hundred street kids and old men and a handful of bikers, soldiers, cops and agents?" He shook his head. "We might as well throw in the towel right now."

"We can't," said Higgins. "We're committed. We've got no choice."

The last truck pulled out of the warehouse.

Hardesty sighed heavily. "What the hell." He shrugged. "I was getting hemorrhoids from sitting on my ass behind a desk, an ulcer from too much lousy coffee and a spare tire from too many fucking jelly doughnuts. I'd just as soon get shot as wait for my damn arteries to close up."

Higgins smiled. "Look at it this way, Jake. We're both a couple of old war dogs past our prime. This here's what you call the last hurrah." He paused briefly. "You got a wife? Kids?"

"Nope," said Jake, his gruff voice like gravel rattling in a can. "Never got around to it."

"Me neither," Higgins said. "I suppose you could say I've got a girl. We had some plans. Nothing real definite. She doesn't know I'm going out with the assault force." He glanced at his watch. "She thinks we're flying out together in about three hours. My security chief's got orders to personally get her out of town, even if he has to tie her up to do it." He snorted. "It probably wouldn't have worked out, anyway."

Hardesty grunted.

Higgins glanced around at the empty warehouse. "Come on," he said. "Let's get the hell out of here."

The battered old Jeep bounced along the pot-holed road through Big Thompson Canyon, heading towards Estes Park. Tracy sat in the back, cradling his battle rifle in his lap, while K.C. sat in the front passenger seat. The driver was her brother, Jase Carter, who had told him that his friends called him J.C.

"Yeah, I know," Karen had said. "K.C. and J.C. And my oldest brother is Tommy Carter, whose friends call him T.C., my old man is Cash Carter, C.C., and my Mom is Mary Jane Carter."

"Don't tell me. M.J., right?"

"You got it. We're a regular alphabet soup."

"Dad thought you were stoned when I told him what you said," said J.C. "And then he heard on the news about Linda Tellerman being arrested by government agents and about your friend being wanted for desertion and shooting down an army chopper. He said, 'Since when does the army send out helicopter gunships to bring back one deserter? Think I'd better have a talk with that boy.' And he sent me out to pick you up."

"That's the first time my father's acknowledged my existence in about four years," K.C. said wryly.

"Why?" asked Tracy.

She stared at him and grimaced. "Why the hell do you think? Dancing in the club is the first *decent* job I've had since I came to Denver. Imagine what I must've done before. Besides, I sorta burned my bridges when I left."

"Let's not talk about that now," her brother said, his eyes on the road. He was in his late twenties, slim, blond like his sister, and dressed in a plaid shirt, jeans, baseball cap and workboots. "I think you're being a little hard on Dad. And Mom cried when she heard you were coming home."

"You're kidding."

"No, I'm serious. She's been blaming herself ever since you left. She wanted us to go and look for you and bring you back, but Dad said no. He said you made your choice of your own free will and we had to respect that. If you wanted to come back, that was up to you."

"Good ole libertarian Dad," said K.C. with a sour grimace.

Tracy felt a little awkward, sitting there listening to family business. He didn't know what had happened to make her leave home and he didn't really want to know. He didn't care what she had done before. All he knew was that she had trusted him and helped him based on nothing but her instincts, and she had taken him in when he was in trouble and fed him and taken risks for him and loved him, and when he told her that he loved her, she had laughed and said she didn't need to hear that. But he had meant it.

He had never been to Estes Park before, but when he saw it, he decided that whatever family trouble K.C. might have had, it must have been pretty serious to induce her to leave such a lovely place. Nestled in a little valley at the entrance to Rocky Mountain National Park and ringed by majestic mountains, Estes Park had once been a resort town that survived primarily by catering to the tourist trade. Old Victorian buildings were interspersed with log homes and more modern construction, among which were some rather tacky fake Swiss chalet-type malls and storefronts, but not even their tastelessness could detract from the overall effect. They drove past the air strip and the hangars the survivalists had built, then through the town, heading toward the stately Stanley Hotel, which stood on a bluff above the town, its columned portico looking out over the valley and affording a breathtaking view of Long's Peak, its summit shrouded in clouds.

The Stanley was a grand old place, built by the man famous for the Stanley Steamer, one of which still stood in its lobby, and immortalized in fiction as the Overlook Hotel by a celebrated horror writer who had stayed there. It was still a hotel, though there were rarely more than a few guests, usually business people from Denver there on a conference or just to relax and get away from the city and soak up some rustic atmosphere.

The town was now an enclave of survivalists and libertarians, rugged individualists who gave the place a paramilitary atmosphere. Stores that had once sold Indian jewelry, rugs and paintings now dealt in various types of ordnance and military equipment. Window displays held AKM rifles, Viper machine pistols, M16s and M60 machine guns, LAW rockets, grenades, semiauto pistols and revolvers and reloading presses and supplies, with components ranging from a wide assortment of powders and full-metal-jacket or military "hardball" rounds to lead-molded bullets and jacketed hollowpoints, flechettes and saboted shot rounds. Surplus military vehicles were plentiful upon the streets, from Jeeps and Hummers to small armored personnel carriers and even a couple of MI tanks, as well as pickup trucks, dirt bikes and even horses in Western tack.

It looked as if the small resort town had been invaded by a horde of motley mercenaries with a heavy sprinkling of rednecks and cowboys. People on the streets wore western clothing complete with sixgun rigs, tiger stripe fatigues and paratrooper boots, lumberjack outfits and jogging suits. There were several small manufacturing concerns in Estes Park, notably the American Small Arms company that produced, among other ordnance, the 9mm. Viper machine pistols and the polymer/ceramic .45 Demon semiautomatics.

Like Texas, Estes Park wasn't really a part of the union, but unlike the Lone Star Republic, it had never formally seceded. The residents of the ultra-capitalist settlement simply refused to pay any kind of taxes, though there was a fund maintained for voluntary contributions to the federal government, which most of the business concerns contributed a part of their profits to. The government of Estes Park consisted of a Town Council and a Peer Review Board. There was no police department, but the citizens volunteered their time to serve on the town posse, which was led by the town marshall, the only fulltime law enforcement officer in the enclave. There was no drug problem, since narcotics of all types were sold freely over the counter to anyone who wished to purchase them, though there was a town ordinance against "public intoxication," applied at the discretion of the town marshall and the Peer Review Board, to control people whose use of intoxicants disturbed the peace. Violators were fined and/or required to perform community service. Habitual offenders and felons were not sentenced to prison, but were completely ostracized. They found themselves unable to work, unable to make any purchases of any sort and unable to socialize. They soon left the community.

The seal of the Estes Park Enclave, its flag and the masthead of its newspaper all bore the image of a coiled rattlesnake, prepared to strike, and the legend "*Laissez Faire*!" That flag, black and red on a yellow background, flew over the Stanley Hotel as they pulled up, signifying that the Town Council was in session. They went through the lobby and turned right, entering the meeting room.

The meeting room was casually informal. There was a bar set up alongside the left wall and comfortable chairs placed around in a sort of loose circle. There was no dais and no table or podium. There were about thirty people present, men and women. The men all looked relentlessly healthy and casually self-possessed; the women looked like free-spirited mountain girls and terrorists. Even the older people in the room had a natural, pioneer sort of glow about them. Tracy had a feeling that at any moment, they would either start repelling an Indian attack or launch into a square dance. One of them, an attractive, long-haired brunette in faded jeans, western boots and a checked flannel shirt, came running up to them and threw her arms around K.C.

"K.C.! Oh, honey, I'm so glad to see you!"

She started crying.

"Hi, Mom."

Tracy was a bit taken aback. The woman looked more like her older sister than her mother. She didn't look a day over thirty. She hugged her daughter tightly and K.C. seemed a little awkward about it, as if she hadn't been prepared for the reaction. A moment later, one of the men came up to her, a little nervously it seemed, and said, "Welcome back, K.C."

There was a moment of uncomfortable silence.

"Hi, Barry." K.C. averted her eyes. She swallowed hard. "How are you?"

"I'm fine, K.C. How are *you*?"

There was a tension between them.

"Okay, I guess."

"Barry and I are married now, K.C.," her mother said.

"Oh," K.C. said in a small voice. "Well . . . congratulations."

"What's in the past is in the past," her mother said. "Okay? Can we just start from that?"

"I . . . I didn't think you'd ever want to see me again," K.C. said.

"We've both been blaming ourselves ever since you left," Barry said. "I really hope you'll stay this time."

Tracy felt like an outsider. He *was* an outsider. But a moment later, K.C.'s mother turned to him and said, "You must be Reese Tracy," she said. She held out her hands. "Welcome."

"Thank you," Tracy said, taking her hands somewhat awkwardly.

"We'll be starting the meeting as soon as Cash arrives," she said. "In the meantime, can I bring you a drink?"

"A beer would be nice," said Tracy.

"Coming right up."

Barry introduced himself briefly, they shook hands and then he excused himself and moved away.

K.C. stared after him for a moment. She had a strange expression on her face.

"What was all that about?" asked Tracy, and the moment

he said it, he regretted it. "Not that it's any of my business, of course...."

"Old wounds," she said. She turned to face him and took a deep breath. "I never thought they would forgive me."

"You don't have to tell me."

"I don't want to keep anything from you, Trace. Although you probably won't think much of me when I tell you. I found out that Mom was having an affair with Barry. I hated her for it. And I hated him. I couldn't tell Dad, but I wanted to hurt them. It's a long story, but I'll make it short and not very sweet. I got him stoned without his realizing it and seduced him. He was so wrecked, he didn't even know what the hell was going on. And I set it up so Mom would walk in on us." She grimaced. "I was fifteen."

Tracy stared at her, astonished. He didn't know what to say.

"Nice, huh? I knew she'd freak out, which she did, but I figured it would break them up, which it didn't. Mom called me a whore, moved out of the house and refused to see me or talk with me again. Dad... he wouldn't even get mad. He said that whatever problems him and Mom were having were between them and none of my business. He said that he could understand my feeling hurt and angry, but that what I'd done was a pretty ugly thing and that I should go to them and try to work it out. I couldn't believe he said that. And I wasn't about to go and apologize. So I just split."

She glanced at him and shrugged. "So that's the whole sordid story of how I wound up on the Denver Strip. Actually, there's more after that, but I figure you've probably heard enough. Anyway, it's been nice knowing you."

"People make mistakes," he said, knowing that it sounded rather lame. "Sounds like everyone in this situation made their share. They seem willing to forgive you. Your mom was right, you know. What's in the past is in the past. It's now that matters."

She sighed. "God, why couldn't I have met you five years ago?"

He smiled. "Like I said, it's now that matters."

Her mother came back with a couple of beers for them. "K.C., there's your father," she said, looking toward the door.

The man who came in looked like Santa Claus out on a

camping trip. Like K.C., his hair was so blond that it was almost white. He wore it longish in the back and he had a huge white-blond beard. He was of medium height, about as tall as Tracy, but he outweighed him by at least a hundred pounds. He was very stocky, with a huge barrel chest and a bit of a paunch, though he wasn't really fat. He came straight over to them.

"M.J.," he said, giving his ex-wife a kiss on the cheek. Then he turned to K.C. "It's good to see you, pumpkin." He gave her an affectionate hug and a kiss. "I really missed you, honey. Welcome home."

She started to tear up.

"Oh, Daddy...."

"It's okay," he said. "You're home now, that's all that matters." He turned to Tracy and held out his hand. "Cash Carter."

"Reese Tracy. Nice to meet you, sir."

"Thank you for bringing my little girl back home," he said.

"Well, I didn't really bring her, sir. She brought me."

"No matter. Anyway, we can talk later. K.C. told me a little about what's happened. And a little was enough to ruin my whole day. What I'd like to do is start the meeting and have you fill everybody in. Can you do that?"

"Yes, sir."

"Good. Let's get this show on the road, then."

Higgins glanced at his watch. They had less than thirty-six hours. Maybe they could extend that if the President called Cord and capitulated. Keep him from going public and starting a mass panic. Jesus, he thought, the government's about to fall and nobody knows about it but a handful of frightened people. He'd spoken to the President over a secure radio channel shortly after he'd arrived at La Guardia. The man had sounded awful. Well, what could he expect? He'd wanted to know how things were progressing, how many people they had, what the status of "the mission" was. *The mission*. What a joke, thought Higgins.

He was standing in a dilapidated hangar on the grounds of a deserted airport, once one of the largest in the country, but now the airstrips were cracked and buckled with weeds growing up through them. And from this unlikely place, they were going to launch a "mission," a certain suicide attempt by a pathetically inadequate band of soldiers, young street crazies and old men. They had gathered together a fleet of assorted old vehicles, jeeps and 4 X 4s and trucks that had been hurriedly equipped with armor plate, pulled all the ordnance they could get their hands on from the armories, drugs and money to pay off the hired so-called talent and three huge C-17's from the Newark base. All things considered, it was a miracle that they had done this well. They had assembled several units of volunteers drawn from troops stationed in the area, and there were the agents and the cops, but it still wasn't enough. Not nearly enough to take on the troops that Cord had under his command. But still, there was a chance, a chance that if they could manage enough of a distraction, Steele could get through and get to Cord . . . or was he only kidding himself?

"What if he launches the missiles the moment the attack starts?" the President had said, in an agony of indecision.

"It's possible, sir, but I don't think he'll do that. He'll probably take one look at our so-called 'assault force' and start laughing himself silly. But if it allows Steele to get through, he'll be laughing out of the other side of his face."

"What if Steele *doesn't* get through?" the President had said, his voice strained. "My God, how can I take such a chance with the lives of all the people in this city?"

"You're not taking that chance, sir. You're going to capitulate. You're going to give in to Cord's demands and do exactly what he tells you to do. You don't know anything about this."

"Jesus, Higgins. . . ."

"If we fail, sir, you'll hand over the government to Cord. There'll be nothing else to do. I know Zach Cord, sir. He may have slipped a cog or two, but I honestly don't believe he really wants to launch the missiles. And I don't think he will unless it's the last option he's got left. If it comes to that, he'll do it, but not until his back is up against the wall."

"But that's exactly what you're talking about doing," said the President, "putting his back against the wall."

"Not really, sir. We're just going to try to get him to turn it for a short while. And, if we're lucky, while his back is turned, we might be able to stop him. If not, then he's won. And if he's won, he won't need to launch the missiles.''

Higgins had tried hard to make the President believe that. He only hoped that he believed it himself. He stepped outside for a breath of fresh air and a cigarette, which, he decided, was an oxymoron if he ever heard one. Hardesty came out with him.

"Got the jitters too, huh?" he said.

"Where the hell is Steele?" Higgins said tensely.

"He'll be here," said Jake Hardesty.

"How long does it take to drive out from Montauk, anyway?" said Higgins with exasperation. "Why the hell couldn't he have flown back?"

"Probably to make sure the people that he got actually came," said Hardesty with a grimace. "You never know what the hell those bikers are gonna do."

"I don't know what the hell *these* people are going to do, either," Higgins said, glancing back toward the hangar. "I wouldn't be surprised if they just grabbed the stuff we've got here and took off."

"If they tried, my men would shoot them and they know it."

"Most of them don't even know what the hell is going on," said Higgins.

"What did Ice tell them?"

"Just that we needed some heavy people to take on some renegade troops."

"Well, that's true, ain't it?"

"Yeah, but they don't know who the troops *are*," said Higgins. "The moment they find out who they're really up against, they're all liable to turn tail and run."

Hardesty shrugged. "So don't tell them. Wait till we get to Wyoming. Then they either have to go for it or walk home."

"You should have been a general," said Higgins.

Linda Tellerman came out to join them. She was wearing a borrowed pair of Strike Force fatigues that were slightly large on her. Her cameraman was right behind her.

"This is crazy, Higgins," she said. "About half those people in there are total head cases. Cord's troops will chew them up. It'll be like the charge of the Light Brigade. Assuming they don't all just drop their weapons and take off for the hills the minute the shooting starts."

"Then maybe you'd better stay behind," said Higgins.

"Hey, forget it. We had a deal. I don't make a stink about being busted and shot up with truth drugs, you take me along to cover the story. Don't try to back out now."

"I'm not trying to back out, Miss Tellerman," said Higgins. "But this was your idea, not mine. After what we put you through, I figured the least I could do was accede to your request. But once we get to Wyoming, you're on your own. I can't guarantee you any protection."

"I didn't ask for any." She frowned. "What is that, thunder?"

"Great, that's all we need," said Higgins. "That hangar roof is full of holes."

"That isn't thunder," Hardesty said, gazing out toward Grand Central Parkway. "It's bikes. A *lot* of bikes."

The sound grew rapidly louder until it became deafening. People started to come out from inside the hangar to see what it was. And then they saw them, winding down the road like some kind of impossibly huge serpent. The Brood, riding in formation.

"Jesus Christ!" said Higgins. "I don't believe it. *Look* at all of 'em!"

"There must be at least five hundred bikes," Hardesty said, amazed.

The air throbbed with the sound of straight pipes. It sounded like an earthquake.

"Mickey, get a shot of this!" said Linda to her cameraman.

The lead bikes entered the airport and came across the buckled tarmac heading toward them. The rider in the lead looked like Death himself, dressed from head to toe in black leather, pale as a ghost, with long white hair flying in the wind, his arms up high on the handlebar grips. Behind him and to the right rode Peacemaker, the Uncle Sam death's head flag of The Brood flying from a pole bolted to the rear of his bike. And next to him rode Steele, wearing a leather motorcycle jacket with Snake's colors over it. They passed in front of the astonished crowd gathered in front of the hangar and the lead three bikes pulled up. Snake held his left arm up, made a circling motion with it and the bikes circled round, peeled off and started to line up on the tarmac. There seemed to be no end to them. The roar of their engines was so loud Higgins had to shout to make himself heard to Hardesty, who was standing right next to him.

"Look at this!" he yelled. "They even brought their own damn fuel!"

Several old tanker trucks painted with the club's colors brought up the rear of the huge formation, as did a small fleet of panel trucks and vans. They pulled up behind the ranks of motorcycles as Peacemaker stood beside his bike, directing the club as it formed up. Then he held his right arm up and pumped it up and down several times. The bikers all revved their throttles as they stood in place, and the sound made the entire hangar shake. Then they shut down.

"Damn," said Higgins. "We've got us a fucking army."

As the bikers started to dismount, Steele came up to them.

"Sorry," he said with a shrug. "This was the best I could do."

Higgins grinned. "You did all right," he said.

Then Steele glanced past him and saw Ice and Raven coming toward him, both wearing black Strike Force fatigues.

"Raven!" He looked at Ice. "What's she doing here?"

Ice shrugged. "Lady got a mind of her own."

"That's right," she said to Steele, "and don't give me any arguments about it. I came along on the assault of the Borodini Enclave and I'm going along on this one."

"This is hardly the same thing," said Steele. "We're not going up against a bunch of mobsters. We—"

"I said I wasn't gonna argue," she interrupted. "Jake's got some female Strike Force officers back there, and I can shoot a gun as well as any of them." She glanced at Linda. "And if she's going, so am I. Besides, if you think I'm gonna sit around and wait for some damn nuke to fall or hear you got yourself blown into scrap metal, you can just forget about it."

Snake and Peacemaker came up to join them. "You let your old lady talk to you like that?" asked Peacemaker.

"I talk any fucking way I please," she snapped. "You got a problem with that, you bring it right here!"

And the next thing the biker knew, there was a commando knife in her hand that seemed to appear from nowhere.

Peacemaker grinned. "Fuckin'-A!" he said, slapping Steele on the back. "I *like* her! She can ride with me."

"She rides with *me*," said Steele. He turned to Higgins and Hardesty. "Gentlemen, I'd like to you meet the chief officers of The Brood. Snake, president, and Peacemaker, sergeant-at-arms." He turned to the bikers. "Oliver Higgins, CIA. And Jake Hardesty, Chief of the NYPD Strike Force."

Higgins held out his hand. Snake took it and reversed it in a biker handshake. Hardesty simply grunted. Snake glanced at him and smiled thinly.

"I brought my *own* strike force," he said.

"I can't thank you enough for coming," Higgins said to Snake. "Damn, I think we just might pull this off!"

"You *think*?" said Snake.

"Look, I don't know exactly what arrangements Steele made with you people," said Higgins, "but whatever the deal you concluded was, I just want you to reassure you that he was fully authorized to—"

"*I'll* tell you what the deal is, man," Snake interrupted. "The deal is we got our own supplies and our own ordnance. The deal is we get to rumble Cobra Force. The deal is you don't tell us *squat*. You just get us there, then get the fuck out of our way. *Got* it?"

Higgins raised his eyebrows and glanced at Steele.

"That's the deal," Steele said.

"Got it," Higgins said.

"Righteous," said Snake. "Now what can you tell us about the layout?"

"Come on inside," said Higgins. "We've got a scale mock-up of the base set up. We'll run the briefing, then load up the planes. We're leaving tonight."

"Mr. President?" said Cord.

"All right, General," the President said, his voice heavy. "You win. There's nothing we can do to stop you."

"I'm glad you're being intelligent about this, sir," said Cord into the phone. "I don't think you'll regret it."

"I'll regret it very much," the President said, "but you've

left me no other choice. You're holding all the cards. Tomorrow morning, I will appear before the Congress and officially announce that I'm surrendering the government to you. I imagine that announcement will cause something of a riot, but once I've explained the situation, I don't think Congress will buck me on this."

"I want that announcement televised," said Cord.

"As you wish."

"And I want to address the nation immediately following your speech," said Cord. "Have the network make arrangements to send up a crew from Denver."

"Very well. You realize, General, that an orderly transfer of authority would involve a very complicated process. In order to minimize the difficulties, I've assembled a committee of experts to fly out and advise you. I hope you will accept them."

"Send 'em on out," said Cord, "but just in case you might have any ideas about an assassination, Mr. President, be advised that your people will be checked out very thoroughly."

"I understand that."

"Good."

"I imagine you'll want my formal resignation."

"I don't think that will be necessary, sir," said Cord. "At least not right away. I intend to use the existing government bureaucracy for the time being. But rest assured that I intend to slim it down. This country's going to be run efficiently. For now, I'd like you to remain in office as my chief executive."

"I'm flattered," the President said wryly. "And what title do *you* intend to use?"

"I think the title 'Provisional Military Governor' would be appropriate."

"Not Caesar?" said the President.

"Save your sarcasm, sir. It's wasted on me. I have no desire to see this country become a totalitarian regime. But until we can get things fully back under control, it will be necessary to institute martial law. Hard times require hard measures."

"Yes, I suppose they do," the President said. "Well, then unless you have any further instructions, I had best go and get to work on my speech. It won't be a very easy one to make."

"I'm sure you'll do fine, sir," Cord said. "I'll be watching. Goodbye."

"Goodbye, General."

Cord hung up the phone and turned to Col. Tyler with a smile. "That's it," he said. "We've taken control of the government without even firing a shot."

"Congratulations, sir."

"Thank you, Seth. The President said he was going to fly out a committee of advisors to help expedite the transfer of authority. And there will be a news crew coming up from Denver. Alert security and make sure they're all thoroughly searched when they arrive. We'll have to prepare quarters for them. And call a full formation for reveille tomorrow morning. I want to announce our victory to the troops. We'll have a busy day ahead of us. But right now, I think we deserve a drink. Will you join me?"

"Thank you, sir. I'd feel honored."

Cord poured them each a whiskey. He raised his glass and Tyler did likewise.

"To the new order," said Cord.

"To the new order," Tyler echoed.

They drank. And as they emptied their glasses, the matrix clone, which had sped through the phone lines from the Federal building, started hurtling through the power lines of the base.

It was about an hour before dawn. The van bearing the news crew from Denver slowed as it approached the three large 4 X 4s blocking the road ahead of them. "Shit, that's all we need," the news reporter said to her driver and camera operator. "Raiders. They'll steal our van and all the equipment and leave us lying in the road. Don't stop, for God's sake! Go around them!"

"I *can't* go around them," said the driver. "They've got the whole damn road blocked off."

"Great," said the reporter. "Maybe they'll only rape me and kill you."

"I don't think they're raiders," said the driver as he saw the men approaching them in the glare of his headlights. "They're wearing uniforms. They look like soldiers."

He slowed to a stop. Steele, Ice and several armed soldiers in battle fatigues came up to their van. Steele opened the passenger side door.

"Would you get out, please?" he said.

"Look, we haven't got much money...."

"Take it easy, Miss, we're not raiders. We're government agents. Please step outside."

"Look, I don't know what this is all about," she said as she got out of the van, "but we're from Channel 4 in Denver, and we're on our way up to Cheyenne to cover an important story. The President is going on the air in a few hours, and we've been asked to provide a live hook-up to—"

"I know all about it, Miss," said Steele. "That's how we knew you were coming." He glanced at the driver. "You the cameraman?"

"That's right."

"Let me have your jacket."

"What is this?" asked the reporter. "What's going on?"

"He's going to show me how to work his rig," said Steele, "then he's going to get in that truck over there and go with these men. And I'll be coming along as your cameraman."

"Whoa, wait a minute! Who the hell are you and what's this all about?"

"The name's Steele, Ma'am. And this is a matter of national security. We're operating under the direct orders of the President of the United States."

"Wait a minute. Donovan Steele? The cyborg?"

"That's right, Ma'am. What's your name?"

"Sheila Blaine."

"Well, Miss Blaine, like I said, this is a matter of national security. I'll brief you fully on the way to Warren, but I'll tell you up front that this is going to be dangerous. I'd really much rather have you go along with the men and let someone take your place, but as a local news reporter, you're face is liable to be known, and that'll help us to get in. If anything goes wrong, I want you to tell them that I forced you into this at gunpoint. You understand?"

She stared at him, then glanced at the soldiers. "What's happening? What are you going to do?"

"We're going to try to prevent a military coup," said Steele. "I'll fill you in on the way, but right now we haven't got much time. Now show me how to use that camera."

# 9

It was still dark when they arrived at the base. They were ordered out of the van at gunpoint by the base security police, and a couple of men immediately went inside to search it. The SP's were all regular personnel, but the sergeant of the guard was wearing a Cobra Force uniform and beret. He beckoned them over to the guard house.

"This way, please."

It felt funny to have the man say "please" when their automatic weapons were pointed at them. They were escorted into the guardhouse.

"I'll have to ask you to strip," said the sergeant. The name tag over his breast pocket gave his name as "Painter."

"I *beg* your pardon?" said Sheila Blaine.

"Corporal Macy...." said Sgt. Painter.

A young female SP stepped forward.

"Corporal Macy will take you into the bathroom, Ma'am," he said. "I'm sorry, but the base is on alert, and we have orders to strip-search all visitors. Please don't make it difficult. We'll try to make it as quick and painless as possible."

"Go ahead, Sheila, it'll be okay," said Steele.

With a sullen look, the newswoman went with Cpl. Macy.

"Okay, buddy," said the sergeant. "Strip."

Steele took off the jacket he had borrowed from the cameraman, with the station logo on it. He was thankful that he had remembered to use his knife to remove the name tag sewn over his breast pocket. He had expected to be searched and he had carried no weapons. At least, none that they'd be able to see. He just hoped that they wouldn't examine him *too* closely. He had to give the President a lot of credit for realizing that Cord wanting a news crew brought in would provide an excellent opportunity for him to slip inside the base. If he managed to pull this off, he'd have to remember to thank the man. Now if only no one recognized him. . . .

The sergeant frowned when he took off his jacket. "Those look like military fatigues," he said.

"Police surplus," Steele said with a shrug. "The station only buys those fancy jumpsuits for the on-camera reporters. These are comfortable on assignment and they got a lot of pockets."

"I see."

"Yeah," he continued as he stripped down. "They had some other guy's name on 'em, so I just tore it off. Listen, you wouldn't know where I could get another one of those tags made up with my name on it, would ya?"

"Why, so you can tell the girls how you saw some action in the service?"

Steele grinned sheepishly. "Yeah, something like that."

The sergeant grimaced. "You wanna-be's make me puke. You all want to dress up and play soldier, but you ain't got the balls to enlist."

"Hey, come on, give me a break," said Steele. "I got a wife and kids."

"So do I," said the sergeant. "Only I'm doin' something to see that my kid gets to grow up in a better country. What's *your* excuse?"

Steele looked properly humble and said nothing. A couple of the other soldiers were going through his clothes. Steele was glad he'd remembered to relieve the cameraman of some of his personal effects, like the roll of black electrical tape, the

Swiss Army knife, the little combination tool with the pliers and the wire cutters and stripper and a few other odds and ends to help make his cover more convincing.

"He's clean."

"All right," Sgt. Painter said. "Bend over."

"What?"

"You heard me. Bend over and spread your cheeks."

"Oh, come *on*, for Christ's sake!"

"I ain't interested in your fuckin' asshole," said the sergeant. "Just anything you might have stuffed up it. Now bend over or I'll *bend* you over."

"Oh, for cryin' out loud...."

"Jaworski...."

Private Jaworski looked stricken. "Oh, jeez, Sarge, do I *haveta*?"

Painter simply glared at him.

"I ain't got any gloves!"

"So you can wash your hands after. Now do it."

"Oh, *man*...."

Steele gritted his teeth as he submitted to the indignity.

"Oh, Jesus...." moaned Jaworski, grimacing with distaste.

"Okay, Jaworski, go wash your little hand," said Painter. "All right, buddy, you can put your clothes back on."

Steele got dressed. Sheila came back out a few moments later, looking furious. She gave Painter a look that would have withered a redwood.

"Can we go now?" she said.

"Yeah, you can go," said Painter. "Anderson, ride in with them."

The SP named Anderson got in the van with them and they drove onto the base. They pulled up in front of one of the brick buildings, and a Cobra colonel came out to meet them.

"My name is Colonel Tyler," he said. "The general won't be ready to see you until after reveille. He's going to address the troops during formation, and I think you'll want to cover that. You need anything to set up?"

"No, we can handle it," said Sheila.

"Well, since you've got some time to kill, would you like some coffee?"

She glanced at Steele. "Yeah, sure, why not?" he said.

Tyler gave him a curious look. "Haven't I seen you before?"

Oh hell, thought Steele.

"John's been on camera," said Sheila. "He doubles as a crime reporter on the Strip. Maybe you saw that piece he did last month on the gay prostitute killings?"

Tyler grimaced. "I must've missed that one," he said wryly. "If you'll follow me, please. . . ."

He turned and started walking toward the officer's mess.

"That was quick thinking," Steele whispered to her.

"I figured it might throw him off if he remembers he saw you on TV," she said. "You should've worn a hat or something."

"Well, it's been a while," said Steele, "but I'll try to stay in the background and keep my head down. You just keep doing all the talking. You're doing fine."

"I'm scared shitless."

"Hang in there. Just have some coffee and make nice with the colonel. Flirt with him. Keep his mind off me."

"I'll try."

Inside the club, they were led to a table. Sheila sidled up to Tyler and smiled prettily. "I've never met an officer in the Cobra Force before," she said. "You must've had some fascinating experiences."

"I've got my share of war stories," Tyler said, smiling back.

"Maybe we could do an interview, add some color to the segment." She gave Tyler some deep eye contact, then turned to Steele. "Johnny, be a love, I forgot my notebook in the van. And why don't you run a quick check on the dish while you're at it? Save some time later."

"Yeah, sure."

He paused briefly at the door and glanced back toward the table. Tyler was sitting with his back to him and Sheila was running her foot along his calf. He smiled, then turned and went out the door. It was almost dawn.

Higgins sat in the cab of the 4 X 4 smoking his twentieth cigarette in a row. He was dressed in ratty-looking denims and a red bandanna around his forehead, with two polymer/ceramic double-action Demon .45s hanging upside down in shoulder holsters beneath his armpits and an AK-47 resting across his lap. He had a harness strapped across his chest holding spare magazines and grenades, and a knife strapped to his leg. Hardesty was behind the wheel, similarly dressed and wearing a baseball cap. He sat smoking his cigar, looking ridiculously calm.

Jesus, thought Higgins, how long has it been since I've done anything like this? Hell, he'd *never* done anything like this. He hadn't been in combat in years, and back then, he'd been properly dressed for it, in battle suit and helmet, not in some redneck trucker outfit. Even with the body armor on under his flannel shirt, he felt naked.

After the briefing, not a few of the "volunteers" had experienced a sudden change of mind and professed a strong desire to leave, but Snake had put a quick stop to that. He had calmly approached the most vocal of the dissenters, smiled and said, "You wanna go?"

"Fuck, yeah, I wanna go! Ain't nobody told us—"

But he had never gotten any farther than that, because Snake had plunged a Bowie knife deep into his stomach and jerked up on it, lifting the man right off the ground. Then he pulled the knife out, watched the man collapse, wiped the blade on his shirt and straightened up without any show of emotion whatsoever.

"All right, he's gone. Anybody *else* wanna go?"

There were no takers.

Crazy, Higgins thought. That fucker was stone cold, hardcore crazy. But he sure knew how to motivate people.

Yet even with the fear of the bikers and being two thousand miles away from home, not a few of the people they'd brought with them had deserted after they'd landed, melting away into the darkness while they were unloading the big C-17s. And, predictably, the bikers had refused to listen to anything he had to say. "*Just get us there and then get the fuck out of our way,*" Snake had said. Higgins hadn't expected to have to take that literally, but that was precisely what the man had meant. He and Peacemaker had their own ideas about how to assault the base, and they weren't interested in anything that Higgins had to say. In fact, Higgins and Hardesty had found themselves taking orders.

"Your people are gonna be the second wave," Snake had

said. "The minute we reach the base perimeter, you hit it. Ice, your group swings in from the left flank; Higgins, you and Hardesty here take the right. Bishop, you and your volunteers come down the middle, right on our heels. And everybody hits it full-tilt boogie. Nobody slows down or stops, got it? *Nobody*. We're gonna need the speed."

"Now wait a minute, Snake," Higgins had said. "You can't expect to attack the base like a bunch of damned Indians on motorcycles, for Christ's sake! We've got to set up interdicting fire and deploy the—"

"Deploy your ass, man. We do it *my* way. Your way'll fuckin' take all day and give 'em a chance to set up. We hit 'em hard and we hit 'em fast. Put the boots to 'em. That's the way to beat superior odds, man. You *psych* 'em. Strike terror into their fuckin' hearts and roll right over 'em."

"You won't be rolling over anybody that way," Higgins had said. "With those damn straight pipes on your bikes, they'll have a field of fire set up to cut you down before you get within a thousand yards of the perimeter."

"I ain't fuckin' stupid, man. You just sit back and watch. I'll show you how it's done."

And that was that. But Snake had thought it out a bit more carefully than Higgins had suspected. He had sent out a party of sappers, their faces blackened with dirt, carrying explosive charges, knives and silenced pistols. Then, under the cover of darkness, the bikers had started *pushing* their motorcycles toward the base. And now Higgins sat there with the "second wave," waiting for the gray light of dawn. Waiting to see if this desperate, crazy gamble would pay off.

"You think Steele got through okay?" he asked Hardesty.

"He got through."

"I wish I had your faith, Jake."

Hardesty grunted. "It ain't faith. I just know Steele."

Higgins tossed his cigarette butt out the open window and squinted through the slit in the armor plate welded to the front of the truck.

Dawn was breaking.

Pvt. Sloane was bored and tired. He hated night sentry duty. Nothing to do but walk his post back and forth all night. He wasn't supposed to be smoking, but fuck it, it was almost dawn and he could hold the butt with his hand cupped around it so the glow wouldn't give him away. He slung his rifle and took out his cigarettes. He stuck one in his mouth.

*"Pssst. Got a light?"*

Sloane spun around, his mouth open. A blade flashed and he felt a sudden, searing pain, as if someone had drawn a white-hot wire across his throat. He tried to scream, but all that came out was a horrible croaking gurgle as the huge Bowie slashed his throat from ear to ear. He collapsed to the ground. The last thing he heard was a soft whisper, saying, "Smokin's hazardous to your health, man."

A bugle sounded. Reluctantly Col. Tyler tore himself away from Sheila. They were kissing against the wall behind the officer's club. He pulled his hand out from inside her open jumpsuit, where it had been fondling her breast, and sighed.

"Shit. That's reveille."

"Is *that* what that was?" murmured Sheila.

He kissed her once more, hard. "We'll have to finish this later, sweetheart. I've gotta go and meet the general. By the way, whatever happened to your cameraman?"

"Oh, he's probably making some last-minute adjustments to the equipment, getting the transmission set up and all that technical stuff."

"He never did bring back your notebook."

"Yeah, I guess he forgot." She smiled. "Too bad, huh?"

Tyler chuckled and kissed her again. "Damn, you're sexy," he said.

"Mmmm, so are *you*."

"We *are* going to finish this," he said.

"Yeah, but you're leaving me for a general," she said, pouting.

"Duty calls. But hold my place."

She dropped her hand down to his crotch and squeezed gently. "Like this?"

"Ohhhh, baby, don't *do* that," he said. "Not now, please, it just ain't fair."

"All's fair in love and war," she said.

"I gotta go." He kissed her again, plunging his tongue deep into her mouth. "Later."

He hurried off.

Sheila's eyes got hard as she wiped her mouth with her sleeve and zipped up her jumpsuit.

"Don't hold your breath, creep," she said.

Sgt. Painter stepped out of the guard house to watch the sunrise. He took a deep breath of the cool morning air and then froze. He stared out at the high desert plain beyond the base perimeter.

"What the *fuck*...."

A motorcycle engine roared to life, the bellow from its straight pipes shattering the stillness of the dawn. Then another, and another, and another... like the thunder of the gods welling up out of the ground. Before him, less than a couple of hundred yards away, was an unbroken line of motorcycles stretching out across the desert. Hundreds of them, as if they had suddenly appeared from out of nowhere.

*"Holy shit!"*

A keening war whoop went up, and the bikes surged forward in a cloud of dust, front wheels pawing at the sky.

Painter turned to run back inside the guardhouse and suddenly a machine pistol opened up from less than thirty feet away, a biker rising up from the ground and spraying bullets, stitching him across the back. Painter was hurled off his feet as the .45 caliber bullets struck him and exited through his chest. And at the moment that he died, a chain reaction of explosions went off as the charges that the sappers had planted took out large sections of the perimeter fencing.

The troops were just starting to form up on the parade ground for Cord's announcement when the explosions went off and the thunder of motorcycle engines filled the air. The Cobras responded instantly, running to repel the attack. The others scattered under shouted commands from their officers, running to get their weapons, but the bikers had already penetrated the base. The guards had all been silently dispatched and there had been no warning. Motorcycles hurtled through the base like two-wheeled missiles, their riders screaming like a horde of attacking Huns and firing at anything that moved.

"All right," said Higgins into his radio. "Hit it! Move! Move! *Move!*"

The trucks surged forward, men with automatic weapons in their beds. As they jounced over the uneven ground toward the base, in four-wheel drive, Higgins saw several planes coming in from the south, winging over the base. As he watched, small black dots came dropping out of the planes. He saw their chutes open as they came gliding in like a flock of kites.

"Jesus, who the hell is *that*?" shouted Higgins over the roar of the truck's engine.

Hardesty glanced at him quickly. "You don't *know*?"

"*No!* They're not part of this operation!"

"You figure Cord's bringing in reinforcements?"

"That's impossible! How the hell could he have known about the assault?"

Hardesty glanced at him again as the truck lurched toward the base perimeter. "You think maybe somebody else had the same idea?"

Higgins shook his head. "But how . . . *Tracy*! It's gotta be!"

As Tracy came gliding in on his parachute, he heard Cash Carter's voice over his helmet radio.

"Son of a bitch! The base is under attack! Looks like they're being hit by raiders!"

Comprehension dawned instantly. "No!" Tracy said. "It's Higgins! It's the CIA!"

"CIA, my ass!" said Cash, gliding in just below him. "It's a goddamn motorcycle gang, for Christ's sake! We're dropping right into the middle of a war!"

"Who cares?" said Tracy, adrenaline trip-hammering through his veins. "They're on *our* side!"

"Shit," said Cash, "this is liable to get real interesting, people."

"Hey, Cash," said Tracy, feeling an exhilaration unlike anything he'd ever experienced before. "If I get out of this alive, I'd like your permission to marry K.C."

"Hell, kid, if we get out of this alive, *I'll* fuckin' marry ya!"

Tracy heard the laughter of the other men through his helmet and his heart soared. It was crazy, but he had never felt so happy.

Cord came barreling out of his mansion, strapping on his holster belt. Tyler was already on the porch when all hell had broken loose.

"What the hell's going on?" demanded Cord.

"We're under attack!" said Tyler.

Suddenly a shot cracked out, and Cord swung around and fell against the door, a bullet through his shoulder. Tyler spun around, clawing his sidearm out of its holster. He saw Sheila's cameraman standing about thirty-five feet away, his arm held straight out. Instinctively, he dropped down and saw the muzzle flash of the compensated 10mm. gun barrel protruding from the man's palm. The bullet whistled just over his head, and he instantly recalled where he had seen that face before. It was on television, all right, but the bastard was no reporter.

*"Steele!"*

He brought up his pistol and, remembering that the cyborg had bullet-resistant polymer skin over his torso, squeezed off three rapid shots, aiming at his face.

Steele felt a bullet whistle past his right ear, then another one grazed his temple, and the third slammed right into the center of his forehead. His head snapped back from the impact as the bullet ricocheted off his nysteel skull casing, and he fell backward.

*"Get out of here!"* Tyler yelled at Cord, but the general was already way ahead of him.

Ignoring the bullet wound in his shoulder, Cord had plunged back into the house the moment he was hit. He ran straight for his desk. He grabbed a machine pistol from inside one of the drawers and a pouchful of magazines, which he slung over his shoulder. He grabbed the phone and stabbed at the buttons, calling the main launch control center.

"This is Cord," he said the moment the phone was picked up. "Implement Thor's Hammer! *Repeat*, Thor's Hammer! Right *now*!"

"Thor's Hammer acknowledged, sir."

Cord slammed down the phone, and pausing to snatch a battle rifle from the wall, he leaped through the rear window of his office, smashing right through the glass. He hit the ground and rolled, wincing from the pain in his shoulder, and immediately started running. Gunfire was erupting all over the base. And glancing up, he saw parachutes in the sky above him.

"*Skeet!*" he said through gritted teeth. "Skeet, you son of a bitch, I'm gonna *burn* your ass!"

The two Cobra missile crew commanders sat down in their chairs inside the LCC the moment the sharp, high-pitched, oscillating note sounded over the speaker system.

"Think it's a drill?" one of them said.

"Fuck if I know," the other said, holding his key. "We'll find out in a minute."

"*Attention, attention,*" came the voice from the main launch control center. "*Thor's Hammer. Repeat. Thor's Hammer.*"

"Holy shit," said the missile crew commander. "The fucking morons called his bluff! This is it!"

The launch control code came on the display.

"Insert keys and turn!" said the missile crew commander.

"Insert keys and turn."

"Enter launch code!"

"Enter... wait a minute."

"What do you mean, wait a minute? Enter launch code!"

"It changed!"

"*What?* What do you mean, it *changed*?"

"Look! It just fucking changed!"

"What the hell...? Fuck it, enter what's on the display!"

"It just changed *again*!"

"What the hell..."

The code changed again. And again. And again. Faster and faster and faster. The numbers started flashing by so quickly they couldn't even read them.

"What the *fuck* is going on?" said the missile crew commander. "What the hell are they *doing* back there?"

"It must be a malfunction...."

"Well, fix it!"

"*How the hell can I fix it? You mind telling me that? What the hell am I supposed to do?*"

"Get on the phone. Call the main launch control center!"

Inside the main launch control center, Cobra Force Major Phillip Hatzenbuehler stared at the consoles, then grabbed Dr. Steven Franks by the back of his neck and spun him around.

"What the hell did you *do*?" he shouted.

"I didn't do anything!" protested Franks.

"What's happening here? Why are those numbers flashing by like that?"

"I don't know," said Franks.

"What the hell do you mean, you don't *know*?"

"It must be a malfunction of some sort, but I've never seen anything like this."

"Well, *fix it*!"

"Sure," said Franks. "How?"

"What do you mean, how? *You're* the fucking expert!"

"I haven't got the faintest idea what's causing this," said Franks. "I'm as much at a loss as you are."

"*You* did this, didn't you, you son of a bitch? You sabotaged the fucking system!"

"I'll tell you the God's honest truth, Major," said Franks. "If I'd *known* how to do this, I would've *done* it. But I don't know what's happening, I don't know how it happened, and frankly, I don't give a damn. But somehow, something's altering the launch codes on the order of about every hundredth of a second, and I haven't got the faintest idea what to do about it. If I didn't know better, I'd swear someone managed to get a virus into the system, but I can't imagine how. It looks like Thor's Hammer isn't going to fall, after all. Gee, that's a damn shame, isn't it?"

Franks grinned.

Hatzenbuehler punched him in the mouth.

Franks fell against the console and brought his hand up to his bloody lip.

"You can hit me all you want, Major, but it's not going to change a thing. There's some sort of weird bug in the system and tracking it down could take days, weeks or even months. I don't know how it happened or why, but I'm not going to look a gift horse in the mouth. You want to try to launch those missiles, be my guest! But even if I knew *how* to help you, I wouldn't. So you can just go to hell!"

The major swore and picked up the phone, but there was no answer at General Cord's house.

The paratroopers opened up with their assault rifles while they were still in the air. The troops below were in chaos. They couldn't even hear their own officers with all the noise going on around them. Motorcycles were roaring all through the camp, as well as trucks full of armed men, firing wildly with their assault rifles and tossing grenades. The invaders were upon them before they had a chance to form any kind of defense. What they had on their hands was a melee, a riot, an every-man-for-himself street fight along the avenues of the base. Men died as they came running out of the barracks. Motorcycles crashed into buildings and slid across the asphalt in showers of sparks from grinding metal, exploding into flames.

Tracy touched down and released his chute. A pickup truck came squealing to a stop in front of him. He brought his HK-94 around, but the men inside didn't fire at him.

"Who the hell *are* you people?"

"Survivalists, from the Estes Park Enclave!" shouted Tracy. "Who are *you*?"

"Federal assault force!"

"From Higgins of the CIA?"

"I'm Higgins!"

"I'm Tracy!"

"I'll be damned! Get in! Where's Cord?"

"I don't—"

"Look out!"

An automatic weapon clattered behind him as Tracy dropped to the ground and Higgins fired his machine pistol out the window of the truck. Tracy looked over his shoulder and saw Pat Summers collapse to the ground, her rifle dropping from her grasp.

"Oh, no...." he said.

*"Come on! Come on! Get in the truck!"*

Tracy jumped up and clambered into the back of the 4 X 4.

"Where's the main launch control center?"

"That way!" shouted Tracy, pointing.

The truck slewed around, laying rubber as Hardesty spun the wheel.

Steele rolled as he hit the ground, his eyes glowing red as his laser designator switched in, the laser turret sliding out through the port in his left hand. He fired as he came up, and the brilliant beam of coherent light lanced out across the distance between him and Tyler, striking the Cobra right between the eyes. Tyler crumpled and fell down the stairs, a corpse before he hit the ground. Steele came up running. He smashed bodily through the door of Cord's mansion. There was no sign of Cord. He went through the lower floor, searching, and then he spotted the broken window.

"Damn...." he said.

Sheila Blaine crawled toward her van, yanked open the door and lunged inside. She went into the back and grabbed the minicam, then went out the back door and started taping. Bullets smashed into the van beside her, and she cried out, dropping to the ground, barely holding onto the camera. She gritted her teeth and got back up, running low for the shelter of the nearest building. This was the story of her career, and she was damned if she was going to miss out on it. This was her ticket to Midtown.

She took up a position at the corner of the officer's mess and started taping as motorcycles screamed past her, trucks spun out, automatic weapons fire erupted all around her and people screamed and ran and fell and died. One of the bikers skidded out and ran right into a tree. She followed with her camera as his body went spinning through the air and fell like a wet dishrag to the ground. And suddenly she found herself pointing her camera at another camera.

She lowered the minicam and stared at the other cameraman while he did the same thing. Crouching beside him was a woman, speaking into a mike. She recognized her at once.

Linda Tellerman, from New York.

They spotted each other, and Linda and her cameraman ran across to her, narrowly avoiding being struck by a jeep as it barreled past.

"What the hell are you doing here?" screamed Sheila. "This is *my* story!"

"Who the hell are *you*?" Linda shouted.

Sheila identified herself.

"Honey, there's plenty here for both of us," shouted Linda. "Where's Steele?"

"I don't know!"

"Well, find him! That's your story! We'll team up for this one, kid. You're going to New York with me!"

"Hot damn!"

"*Go!* And keep your head down!"

Cord made it to the NCO club and plunged through the door, firing at a biker who came barreling down on him. The biker was blown right off his wheel and fell, bleeding, to the ground while his motorcycle continued on without him to crash headlong into an adjacent building, roaring like a wounded beast.

Cord ran to the phone and called the launch control center.

"Cord here," he said. "Did you implement Thor's Hammer?"

"We *can't* sir," Hatzenbuehler said.

"What the hell do you mean, you *can't*?"

"We've got some kind of malfunction. The system's gone completely haywire. We can't launch."

*"Damnit!"* Cord tore the phone out and hurled it across the room. He stood there, breathing heavily, bleeding from his wound, refusing to admit defeat. And then he realized that he still had a hole card. He ripped the empty magazine out of his machine pistol, slapped in a fresh one and went to the door, checked around, and took off running, heading toward the train alert shelters.

Raven rode in the truck beside Ice, firing her assault rifle through the window. As they slid around the side of one of the buildings, she spotted Steele dropping down out of a window.

"It's Steele!" she shouted. "Stop!"

Ice brought the truck to a sliding stop in front of Steele.

"You get Cord?" Ice said.

"No, he got away," Steele said, jumping up onto the running

board. Ice handed him a machine pistol and gunned the truck forward. "I wounded him, though."

"Can't have gone far," said Ice. "Keep a lookout."

"Who the hell are those people who parachuted in?" asked Steele.

"Damn if I know," Ice said, sliding the truck around sideways as they came under fire from some soldiers concealed in a building. Steele sprayed the windows with the machine pistol as they raced past. "Some party, huh?" said Ice with a grin.

"You're enjoying this, aren't you?" Steele said.

"Damn straight. I havin' me a *fine* time!"

"You're a sick man, Ice."

"Watch it!" Raven shouted.

They swerved and narrowly avoided three bikers, but their speed was too great, and as the truck went sideways, it overbalanced and rolled. Steele was thrown clear. The truck rolled over three times and came to a rest on its side. Steele got to his feet and ran over to the battered vehicle.

"Are you all right?" he yelled.

Raven was crumpled up against the door, moaning. "Banged my head," she said. "Think I'm okay, though."

Ice was bleeding from a big gash in his forehead and several cuts on his face. "Man, what happened?"

A motorcycle came roaring up behind Steele. He turned and saw it was Snake.

"We got 'em on the run, man!"

"Get out of there," said Steele. "The truck could catch fire."

"Yo, man," said Snake, "didja know a fuckin' train just pulled outta here?"

Steele turned. "A *train*?"

"Yeah, came outta a big garage or somethin'."

"The rail garrison!" Steele said. "*Cord!* There's missiles on that train!"

"*Go!*" said Ice.

"Get on!" said Snake. "We'll catch the sumbitch!"

Steele hopped on behind the biker and Snake roared off in pursuit of the rail garrison train.

• • •

Hatzenbuehler heard automatic weapons fire behind him and turned to see Higgins, Hardesty and Tracy coming through the door along with several other men. He pulled his pistol from its holster, but Franks cried out, *"No!"* and lunged at him, knocking the pistol up.

The shot went wild and the Cobra spun around, knocking Franks back and shooting him as he fell back against the console. Then his body jerked as Higgins fired his assault rifle and he fell dead to the floor. The other people in the control room all stood with their hands raised high above their heads.

Tracy came running over to Franks, but one look at the wound told him it was lethal.

"Doctor Franks. . . ." he said.

"It's you," said Franks, blood frothing at his mouth. "You did it! You warned them!"

"Yes, sir, I warned them. Thanks to you."

"Good boy," said Franks. And the life went out of his eyes.

Higgins glanced at the screen and saw the rapidly changing launch code numbers flashing by at incredible speed. He had only seen computers act that way once before.

"No. . . ." he said, in a low voice, "It couldn't have. . . ."

One of the other scientists came up to him. "Cord tried to launch the missiles," he said, "but the launch codes suddenly started changing, all by themselves. I can't account for it. I just don't understand what happened."

Higgins stared at him, then looked back at the screen. He sat down at the console. Could it be. . . . ?

He entered, "Higgins to Matrix, please respond."

Suddenly, the numbers stopped flashing past. And instead of numbers, letters appeared on the screen.

*"Matrix to Higgins. Are you in control of the base?"*

"I'll be damned," Higgins said in a low voice.

"What is it?" Hardesty asked.

Higgins ignored him. He entered, "Base under control. Threat neutralized."

The message came back, *"Nice work. Thought you'd never get here."*

Higgins sat back in the chair, staring at the screen.

"What the hell was *that* all about?" asked Hardesty.

Higgins smiled. And then he started laughing.

The Harley flew over the uneven terrain, Snake fighting to keep it under control, motocrossing the big bike with considerable skill as they gained on the missile train.

"Come on, come on!" shouted Steele. "If he gets up to speed, we'll lose him!"

"Keep your shirt on, I'll get him," Snake said.

Inside the train, Cord locked down the controls and raced back to the missile launch control car. He was weak from loss of blood, but he forced himself to keep on going. He wasn't going to let Skeet Higgins beat him. Not some damn office bureaucrat! He staggered into the launch control car and lurched up to the console.

"Awright, get ready!" Snake shouted.

He was pulling even with the rear of the train.

Steele got up on the footpegs, hanging onto Snake's shoulders as the bike bounced over the uneven terrain.

"Get in closer!"

"Hang on, man...."

They pulled in close....

He'd have only one chance. Steele took a deep breath and put one foot up on the seat, then launched himself at the train. The force of his jump caused Snake to lose control and bike and rider tumbled to the ground, rolling over and over. Steele clamped his fingers onto the railing of the maintenance car and held on for dear life. He glanced behind him and saw Snake staggering to his feet. The biker held up his arm, his hand closed in a fist, and stabbed it out toward him. Steele climbed up the onto the roof of the car just as the launch platform was deployed. Wind bit at him as he ran across the cars. He reached the launch control car, leaped across, dropped down and started ripping his way through the roof.

Cord looked up from the console and brought up his machine pistol. Steele's laser cycled and a bright, pencil-thin beam of light lanced down through the roof at Cord, striking him squarely in the heart. The machine pistol fired as Cord's finger tightened reflexively on the trigger and then he collapsed against the console. Steele dropped down into the car and checked the body. Cord was dead. He exhaled heavily, with relief.

"Okay," he said to himself. "I've stopped the war. Now all I've got to do is figure out how to stop this goddamn train."

# _EPILOGUE

It was, to say the least, a very bizarre wedding reception. It was held in the banquet room of the Stanley Hotel, and the guests were practically all walking wounded. There were bikers in full regalia, wearing slings and head bandages and casts; soldiers in military uniforms with bloody bullet holes still in them; cops in Strike Force battle fatigues, hobbling on crutches; street gang members in their psychedelic Watusi colors carried in on litters because there weren't enough wheelchairs to go around in the entire state of Colorado; battle-scarred survivalists in varied forms of dress, from camo-fatigues to rodeo flash, replete with turquoise jewelry, silver collar tips and toecaps; junkies nodding out and feeling absolutely no pain whatsoever because they'd finally found Nirvana in the town of Estes Park, where drugs could be purchased over the counter as cheaply as beer and cigarettes.

The bride wore a white rodeo queen outfit, fringed western mini-skirt, white high-heeled boots and silk and sequined western blouse studded with rhinestones, with a long white silk bandanna. The groom wore a similar western outfit he had borrowed from the bride's brother, which consisted of hand-tooled western boots made out of bullhide, sky-blue cavalry twill slacks with matching western-yoked jacket, silk shirt and brocade vest and a white Stetson.

The minister who performed the ceremony was Snake, who, to everyone's amazement, turned out to be a Jesuit—or so he claimed, anyway, and no one felt disposed to argue with him. And he did conduct the ceremony properly, so perhaps he really was a priest, for all they knew. As Hardesty grumbled in an aside to Higgins, "Never can tell *what* those Jevvies are liable to do."

Linda Tellerman was maid of honor, and Higgins served as the best man. And Sheila Blaine, who was finally going to New York, taped the entire ceremony as a capper color segment for the network news. And following the brief formal reception, the bride and groom were given a motorcycle escort to their honeymoon lodge by a stream in Rocky Mountain National Park, after which the entire wedding party and most of the population of the town of Estes Park repaired to the airport hangars for a biker-style funeral that turned into a four-day beer blast. Those who had died, and there were many, were given a rousing send-off with a joyful noise that echoed throughout the entire valley. At some point, the President tried to call and congratulate the heroes, but something was lost in translation when a drunken biker answered the call from the Chief Executive, listened for about thirty seconds, slurred, "Suck my dick," and then hung up.

"What I don't understand," Steele said to Higgins, as they watched Peacemaker shooting beer cans from off a petrified prospect's head with his newly acquired Colt Single Action Army, "is why the launch command sequence broke down. Some of the missile scientists told me that Cord ordered the strike, but the computers went haywire for some reason. What happened?"

"I don't know," said Higgins, "some kind of equipment malfunction, I guess. Or maybe an error in computer programming. One of those scientists might have deliberately programmed some kind of glitch into the system. We'll probably never really know."

"Mmmm," said Steele thoughtfully. "Who's Matrix?"

Higgins glanced at him, his eyes and his expression giving nothing away. "Matrix?"

"Yeah. Jake said something about you communicating with somebody called Matrix over the launch control center's console."

"Oh, that," said Higgins. "Jake must've got confused. I was merely trying to interrogate the system, see if I could figure out what the hell the status was. I was scared to death that we might have a launch, but the damn thing was completely on the fritz. Gave me some kind of joke answers. That's what makes me think one of the scientists sabotaged the program. It was probably Franks. And he paid for it with his life, poor bastard."

"But think of all the lives he saved," said Steele.

"Yeah. The man died a hero."

Higgins silently breathed a deep sigh of relief. He wasn't yet ready to explain to Steele about the matrix clone. He wasn't sure if he would ever be. It wasn't Franks who saved the day, but Steele. A duplicate, electronic Steele that had traveled two thousand miles through the phone lines on its own initiative and was now loose somewhere in the country's electronic net. It was everywhere and nowhere. How the hell was he going to explain that?

"Well, after this, Carman will probably have no choice but to reinstate your budget," Steele said.

"Good thing, too," Higgins replied. "You look ridiculous walking around with that bullet hole in your forehead."

"I don't know. Peacemaker said he likes it. I believe he said that it was 'bitchin'.'"

"Yeah, well, he's got a hole in his head, too. Where his brain oughta be."

They watched the huge biker cock the gun, then let off a shot that smashed the beer can on the miserable prospect's head, showering him with foam. Raven came up to them and shook her head.

"Look at that," she said. "Hard to believe those psychos saved the future of this country."

"Oh, I don't know." Steele smiled. "That sorta looks like fun. Hey, Peacemaker," he called out, "mind if I have a shot?"

"Fuckin'-A! Be my guest! Prospect! Another can!"

With a look of silent suffering, the young prospective member of The Brood, who didn't yet know that he was about to be presented with his colors in an initiation ceremony that the club had planned, placed another beer can on his head and closed his eyes.

With a soft whine, the laser turret extruded through its gunport in Steele's left hand and his eyes glowed with twin red dots. A bright beam of collimated light lanced out toward the prospect and burned a neat little hole in the exact center of the beer can. The amber fluid trickled down onto the prospect's face.

"Aw-*right*!" yelled Peacemaker. He brought up the Colt and snapped off a shot, blowing the leaking beer can off the prospect's head.

"Terrific," Higgins said wryly. "We blow several million dollars on that laser battle mod and you use it as a hi-tech can opener."

"Spin-off technology," said Steele with a grin.

Raven rolled her eyes. "Christ. I'm gonna get a beer."

# HIGH-TECH, HARD-EDGED ACTION!
## All-new series!

__ **STEELE** J.D. Masters 1-55773-219-1/$3.50
Lt. Donovan Steele—one of the best cops around, until he was killed. Now he's been rebuilt--the perfect combination of man and machine, armed with the firepower of a high-tech army!

__ **COLD STEELE** J.D. Masters 1-55773-278-7/$3.50
The hard-hitting adventures of Lt. Donovan Steele continue.

__ **FREEDOM'S RANGERS** Keith William Andrews 0-425-11643-3/$3.95
An elite force of commandos fights the battles of the past to save America's future—this time it's 1923 and the Rangers are heading to Munich to overthrow Adolf Hitler!

__ **FREEDOM'S RANGERS #2: RAIDERS OF THE REVOLUTION**
Keith William Andrews 0-425-11832-0/$2.95
The Rangers travel back to the late 18th century to ensure that Washington is successful.

__ **TANKWAR** Larry Steelbaugh 0-425-11741-3/$3.50
On the battlefields of World War III, Sergeant Max Tag and his crew take on the Soviet army with the most sophisticated high-tech tank ever built.

__ **SPRINGBLADE** Greg Walker 1-55773-266-3/$2.95
Bo Thornton—Vietnam vet, Special Forces, Green Beret. Now retired, he's leading a techno-commando team—men who'll take on the dirtiest fighting jobs and won't leave until justice is done.

__ **THE MARAUDERS** Michael McGann 0-515-10150-8/$2.95
World War III is over, but enemy forces are massing in Europe, plotting the ultimate takeover. And the Marauders—guerrilla freedom fighters—aren't waiting around for the attack. They're going over to face it head-on!

---

Check book(s). Fill out coupon. Send to:
**BERKLEY PUBLISHING GROUP**
390 Murray Hill Pkwy., Dept. B
East Rutherford, NJ 07073

NAME_____
ADDRESS_____
CITY_____
STATE_____ZIP_____

PLEASE ALLOW 6 WEEKS FOR DELIVERY.
PRICES ARE SUBJECT TO CHANGE WITHOUT NOTICE.

POSTAGE AND HANDLING:
$1.00 for one book, 25¢ for each additional. Do not exceed $3.50.

| | |
|---|---|
| BOOK TOTAL | $____ |
| POSTAGE & HANDLING | $____ |
| APPLICABLE SALES TAX (CA, NJ, NY, PA) | $____ |
| TOTAL AMOUNT DUE | $____ |

PAYABLE IN US FUNDS.
(No cash orders accepted.)

# HIGH-TECH ADVENTURES BY BESTSELLING AUTHORS

## \_\_TEAM YANKEE by Harold Coyle
0-425-11042-7/$4.95
Live the first two weeks of World War III through the eyes of tank team commander Captain Sean Bannon, as he and his soldiers blast their way across the war-torn plains of Europe.

## \_\_AMBUSH AT OSIRAK by Herbert Crowder
0-515-09932-5/$4.50
Israel is poised to attack the Iraqi nuclear production plant at Osirak. But the Soviets have supplied Iraq with the ultimate super-weapon . . . and the means to wage nuclear war.

## \_\_SWEETWATER GUNSLINGER 201 by Lt. Commander William H. LaBarge and Robert Lawrence Holt  1-55773-191-8/$4.50
Jet jockeys Sweetwater and Sundance are the most outrageous pilots in the skies. Testing the limits of their F-14s and their commanding officers, these boys won't let anything get in the way of their fun!

## \_\_WILDCAT by Craig Thomas  0-515-10186-9/$4.95
Crossing the globe from Moscow to London to East Berlin to Katmandu, the bestselling author of *Winter Hawk* delivers edge-of-the-seat suspense spiked with state-of-the-art espionage gadgetry.

---

Check book(s). Fill out coupon. Send to:

BERKLEY PUBLISHING GROUP
390 Murray Hill Pkwy., Dept. B
East Rutherford, NJ 07073

NAME_____

ADDRESS_____

CITY_____

STATE_____ZIP_____

**PLEASE ALLOW 6 WEEKS FOR DELIVERY.
PRICES ARE SUBJECT TO CHANGE
WITHOUT NOTICE.**

POSTAGE AND HANDLING:
$1.00 for one book, 25¢ for each additional. Do not exceed $3.50.

BOOK TOTAL  $\_\_\_\_

POSTAGE & HANDLING  $\_\_\_\_

APPLICABLE SALES TAX  $\_\_\_\_
(CA, NJ, NY, PA)

TOTAL AMOUNT DUE  $\_\_\_\_

PAYABLE IN US FUNDS.
(No cash orders accepted.)